He doesn't know I know, she realized. He must have not seen her the night before. He was still trying to con her with his cocky Mr. Nice Guy act. For all she know, Loki was waiting just out in the hall. They probably thought they had her cornered then and there—off guard and by surprise. But they were very, very wrong.

"Gaia, are you—"

"I *know,* Josh," Gaia interrupted him coldly. "I know who you work for, and I know what you've been doing to Sam, so you can just drop it."

Josh's grin returned. Then he shrugged. "Okay," he said simply. "Have it your way." He pulled his right hand from behind his back—revealing a nine-millimeter pistol with a four-inch silencer. "This is easier, anyway. I don't have to make nice to such a ball-busting bitch. It's harder than you think."

Gaia's leg muscles tensed. Adrenaline shot through, pumping her body with the electric, pre-combat fizz. She welcomed the sensation. It was like a taste of something sweet and long-forgotten. She could kick that gun away from him and snap his neck in two before he even had a chance to exhale a dying breath.

"I wouldn't try anything," Josh added calmly.

As if on cue, the suite door came crashing open, and three burly men burst into the common room—all clad in black, all brandishing pistols. Before Gaia could make a move, the three muzzles were aimed at her head.

For orders other than by individual consumers, Pocket Books grants a discount on the purchase of **10 or more** copies of single titles for special markets or premium use. For further details, please write to the Vice-President of Special Markets, Pocket Books, 1260 Avenue of the Americas, New York, NY 10020-1586, 8th Floor.

For information on how individual consumers can place orders, please write to Mail Order Department, Simon & Schuster Inc., 100 Front Street, Riverside, NJ 08075.

LOVE

FRANCINE PASCAL

POCKET PULSE

New York London Toronto Sydney Singapore

To Anita Elliot Anastasi

An *Original* Publication *of* POCKET BOOKS

POCKET PULSE, published by
Pocket Books, a division of Simon & Schuster, Inc.
1230 Avenue of the Americas, New York, NY 10020

Produced by 17th Street Productions,
an Alloy, Inc. company
151 West 26th Street
New York, NY 10001

Cover photography by St. Denis. Cover design by Russell Gordon.

ISBN: 0-7434-1252-4

First Pocket Pulse Paperback printing November 2001

10 9 8 7 6 5 4 3 2 1

Printed in the U.S.A.

I've realized that I can sum up my entire life with the statement of two very simple facts. And when presented together, they are so ironically juxtaposed that they are either sickening or hysterical. They are proof positive—as if proof were needed—that my life is nothing more than somebody's cruel joke.

Fact #1: I am fearless.

Fact #2: I am always running away.

There you have it: the sum total of my existence, Gaia Moore in a hermetically sealed nutshell. Pathetic, isn't it? A fearless girl who runs away? It's on par with being a stunningly beautiful girl who has to wear a paper bag over her head or an investment-banking billionaire who lives in a trailer park.

But let's be clear here. True, I can't feel fear. This is not the same thing as being brave, however. It's not like I see myself in some Roman epic, weighted down with a hundred pounds of armor, taking on fifty lions or re-creating a glorious battle. I'm no gladiator. Gladiators *were* brave. Because being brave necessarily means being able to experience fear and then being able to overcome it.

But then, that's my problem, isn't it? I'm not just fearless. I'm "braveless," too.

At the very least, you'd think this little fluke in my genetics would enable me to stay in one place for a while. If I'm not afraid of anything, why the hell should I ever have to run away, right? To that end, fearlessness shouldn't prevent me from making a true friend, either. Or actually *keeping* a true friend. Or falling in love and staying in love. I should be able to stand my ground. I should be able to face every single crisis and tragedy in my life with complete confidence. Running away is for weak-minded cowards.

I tell myself these things.

And then I tell myself: *bullshit.*

Because when you get right down to it, going on the run isn't about fear or bravery. It's about the one principle that applies to every creature on this planet—from the bravest lion to the lowest forms of life, like my father or cockroaches: survival. Self-protection and self-preservation. Even the most fearless animals have a survival instinct. It's what enables them to perpetuate their species. To multiply.

And I can't be any different.

Although I have to be honest: I don't really see myself multiplying in the future. In fact, I'd say the odds of my extinction are increasing by the hour.

Add to that
his hungry,
dark yellow
grin, and
you had the
world's most
foul-
smelling
vampire
pervert.

all that blood

Trail of Bread Crumbs

I NEED TO FOCUS.

Thoughts were smeared like tar inside Gaia's head. Shapeless ideas were flooding her mind, melting together too quickly and hardening into an impenetrable black sludge.

Where am I? What do I know for sure?

The subway car lurched suddenly, taking a wicked turn at a high speed. Gaia bumped her head against the Plexiglas window behind her. She tried to steady herself on the hard, burnt orange plastic seat. The sound of screeching metal needled her eardrums. A thick film of sweat drenched her back, shoulders, and face—causing her brown dress to stick to her like a wet tissue. Her hair was in clumps, glued to the sides of her cheeks.

She had no idea how long she'd been on the deserted train. She wasn't even sure which line this was. She knew she was waking up from one of her postbattle blackouts.

But how long ago had she slipped into unconsciousness?

And where the hell was she, anyway?

She looked across the aisle at the bold white letter encased in a bright blue circle. *C. I'm on the C train. Somewhere in Brooklyn, I think. Need to focus.* Her eyes wandered to the mirrored siding of the train's interior. Her muscles tensed. This in no way helped her to focus. Quite the opposite. Her reflection was divided into blurry stripes: some clear, some opaque, all completely distorted—a cubist painter's urban nightmare. Finding herself in the reflection was next to impossible.

Okay. She had to start from the present and work backward. That was the only solution: to follow the trail of disjointed memories back through time. . . like Hansel and Gretel. And bread crumb by bread crumb, the recent past began to materialize. A flash of running. The terrified look on Sam's face as they fled the Bubble Lounge. Sam's RA, Josh. Then there were Sam's insistent warnings—forcing Gaia to run for safety through a maze of back alleys.

Each new memory was like a sharp kick to the abdomen—even more painful as it settled into her mind's eye, making it unexpectedly difficult to breathe. She and Sam had barely spoken a word in their last moment together on the street. Just a few sentences and one kiss. There hadn't been time for anything else. But finally Gaia understood. Sam hadn't turned on her, as she'd thought for so long. `Someone had taken control of him.` And judging from the look in his eyes at dinner, that "someone" hadn't just taken control; they'd scared him in a way that had changed him, maybe for good. There wasn't even a word for that kind of fear. Not one that Gaia knew, anyway.

But one thing was certain. Whoever had chased Gaia down those side streets must have been terrorizing Sam for months—all those months that he'd been such a bleary-eyed ghost of himself. *Months.* And all to get to her. Sam had said as much on the street: "*It's you they're after.*" Her stomach twisted. She cringed in shame. *She* had brought Sam into her relentlessly miserable existence. And for that, he'd been—well, who knew what? Blackmailed? Tortured? Worse? All for loving and trusting her. All for wanting to protect her.

She sniffed, her eyes flashing back to the dark subway tunnel. She was to blame. For everything. For all the changes in Sam, for the stilted conversations and fights, for all that mistrust and poisonous distance. It was all her fault. Right from the start. Even their breakup, even the fact that she no longer loved him the way she once had. . . yes, that was her fault as well. The thought of it was almost too twisted to face—too complicated and tragic even for her. The guilt was a hydraulic press. It crushed her entire body from both sides. She knew she still loved him somehow, in some way, but it would never be the same as it was. They had successfully destroyed that original emotion. Whoever the hell they were.

But at least now they'll leave him alone, she tried to

reassure herself. The train slowed. She nodded and wrapped her arms tightly around her chest for warmth. That was the only solace she could take from this nightmare: Sam would finally be able to start living his life again, without the curse of Gaia Moore hanging over his head. They couldn't possibly use him now that Gaia knew the truth—that they had used him to get to her. He served no purpose anymore. They'd failed.

She nodded again. She could take some comfort in that. But that feeling was quickly muted by flashes of disturbingly bleak violence. More images slashed through her mind like jump cuts from some disgusting gory movie. Those two thugs who had followed her onto the train. . .

All that blood.

The fight had taken place on the A train; she remembered that. She must have switched over to the C right before she passed out. Bile rose in her throat. She'd blown open one of the guys' kneecaps with his own gun. But he had actually offed himself before she could get any information out of him. He must have known he was as good as dead after screwing up Gaia's capture. Which meant, of course, that death was preferable to actually facing his boss and admitting failure.

And that's when it hit her—as hard and fast as the gunshot to his knee. She slid back on her seat and crammed the palms of her hands into her eye sockets, trying to jump-start her dormant brain cells. Somehow she had skipped over the abundantly obvious. She'd been too distracted by the chaos and blood on that train.

The man's boss was Loki.

Of course. Only he could be so fearsome, so intimidating. This was how Loki operated—using people like chess pieces in his own vast game, every little maneuver designed to inch closer to his opposing queen. Which would be her. But why? Why was he doing this? What could make him despise Gaia so much that he would go to such lengths to destroy not just her life, but any life she touched?

And more important: who *was* Loki?

If she listened to her uncle, it was her father. If she listened to her father, it was her uncle. It was an endless game of tug-of-war between two men she could never trust. Sam's strange words at dinner came floating back to her: all that stuff about what a great guy her uncle was. Did that mean Oliver was Loki? Was he feeding Sam the lines? Forcing Sam into luring Gaia to him? Or maybe they *weren't* lines. If her father was Loki, then maybe Oliver was trying to send her a message through Sam—trying to get her safely away from her father. Maybe her father had never even left New York. He could have just gone into hiding, watching her, waiting for the right moment to strike. And what if her father was the one who was talking to Sam? How would Sam even know the difference? The endless questions were burning holes into the lining of Gaia's skull.

But her thoughts were cut short as the train pulled into the next stop.

The doors opened. A disgustingly filthy man boarded the train and—given the choice of every other empty seat on the car—proceeded to sit down right next to her.

Gaia's jaw tightened. *Of course.*

His once white sweatshirt was almost entirely black, as was his wool hat. They matched his soiled black beard and eyebrows. The stench alone was almost enough to make Gaia pass out again; he reeked powerfully of alcohol and stale sweat. Add to that his hungry, dark yellow grin, and you had the world's most foul-smelling vampire pervert. Without hesitating, Gaia shot up from her seat and moved down to another. He followed. He sat down, rubbing his thigh against hers. Once again he slid as close as possible, widening his drunken grin. And then he spoke, spewing out an indescribable stink with each slurred word: "You show pity."

Gaia almost flinched. Obviously he had meant to say, "You're so pretty." But the former version was strangely unsettling. Maybe because it wasn't true. She didn't show pity; she didn't even *feel* pity. Certainly not toward this man. She felt only rage. But she told herself that she'd simply ignore him and bolt for the doors at the next stop. She didn't need to expend any more energy right now.

Then he grabbed her. His hand clamped down on her inner thigh. The grip was surprisingly strong. Without a moment's thought Gaia snapped his hand from her thigh and began to crush the bones of his fingers with every ounce of her strength. The perverted smile dropped instantly from his face as he let out a pathetic tortured moan and stared pleadingly into Gaia's eyes. It never ceased to amaze her how quickly these assholes turned into little boys at the first sign of pain. Gaia stared back at him with nothing but cold rage. His desperate eyes meant nothing to her right now. He wasn't even a person to her at this moment. He was just a symbol. A symbol for all of them.

She increased the pressure to his hand, watching his entire arm begin to shake as beads of sweat turned into black rivulets streaming down his filthy face and neck. This poor scumbag had no idea what he'd just walked into. He had no idea what Gaia felt like doing to him at this moment—to all the faceless sadists who wouldn't leave her alone, who never gave her a moment's peace in her life. Maybe she'd go ahead and break each and every individual bone in his body.

Send them all a message. She could feel her rage about to take over completely, all the lessons of honor and necessary force right out the window. No one else played by the rules; why should she? She gazed deeper into his shit-colored eyes, aching to rip him apart. . . when something in his expression changed.

The shift was so subtle, she barely even noticed, but somehow his grimace had begun to even out. . . into a smile. What the hell was he smiling about? Was he unaware that Gaia was about to permanently dismantle his hand? Had he finally lost all the feeling in it?

"You like that, don't you?" he whispered knowingly, running his tongue across his rotting front teeth. The look of recognition increased in his eyes as he stared Gaia down with a new and disturbing confidence. "Bad girl," he slurred, leaning toward her with an almost menacing giggle. "You've been a bad girl." His giggles were turning into hearty, phlegm-ridden laughs.

Gaia dropped his hand and took a huge step back, searching deeper into his crazed eyes. Something in those disturbed but knowing eyes. . . What was it? Watching him laugh in her face, Gaia was ninety-nine-point-nine percent sure he was nothing more than a psycho pervert train dweller. But now, after everything she'd learned on this interminable night, there was a new possibility—however infinitesimal it might be—that he was something far more dangerous. Now Gaia realized that every single man or woman in her vicinity. . . could be one of Loki's people. Every cabdriver, waiter, and store clerk was a potential plant. Every anonymous suit with a cell phone and every bum. That was how Loki worked. And in that brief moment, staring into the sinister eyes of that sicko, whether he was the real thing or not, her sense of imminent danger had just quadrupled. It was no longer just an inkling or a bad vibe, it was something Gaia knew: she had to get the hell off of that train and run.

As the train pulled into the Fulton Street station in Manhattan, Gaia kicked into high gear. The pervert took one last step toward her, but she snapped out her leg with a pinpoint side kick to his jawbone, sending him instantly to the floor. She ripped the wool cap from his head and leaped between the closing doors out onto the platform. She took each staircase with two leaps, jumping over the exit turnstile and finally reaching aboveground. The sky was still dark. She must not have been out for that long. A quick glance at the digital clock of a bank told her it was only a few minutes after midnight. She stuffed her matted blond hair—her most identifiable feature—under the filthy wool cap. The gusts of cold wind felt twice as deadly against her naked shoulders and sweat-drenched dress, but that didn't stop her from launching into a full-fledged gallop heading uptown on Water Street.

If she wasn't running, she wasn't safe. She knew that now.

Loki could be anywhere and everywhere. For all she knew, Loki could have been responsible for every single violent encounter she'd ever had in New York City. He'd probably been watching her every move since day one. He'd had Ella under his thumb and now Sam. He could invade Gaia's personal life at will. He could mess with anyone he pleased, and that meant no one was safe.

Not that she hadn't felt it a thousand times before, but now it was official: Gaia Moore was poison to anyone remotely close to her. She had to leave them all behind. She didn't just need to hide, she needed to disappear immediately—to go deep undercover. No time to say good-bye to Paul and the other Mosses. No time to say good-bye to Sam or even alleviate her guilt by thanking him for all the sacrifices he'd obviously made. Besides, Sam would probably be ecstatic to finally have Gaia out of his life for a while. No time even to say good-bye to Ed...

Gaia suddenly found herself stopping in the middle of street, though she wasn't sure why. It was almost involuntary. Like her body knew things that her mind didn't. Had there been any cars on the road, she would have been mowed down. She bent over and clung to her knees for support, gasping for air and ignoring the razor-sharp cramps in her stomach. *Run, goddammit!* she chided herself. *What the hell are you stopping for?*

Her frustration mounted with every additional

second she stood still, but she needed those few seconds to answer her own question. Ed. Ed was the reason she'd stopped running. What was it? Was it the thought of abandoning him—a sudden image of Ed alone that made her stop? Or was it the thought of not having him—of not having the one true friend she'd ever made in this life besides Mary? Leaving Ed without some kind of good-bye. . . it was simply too cruel. Sam knew the kind of danger Gaia was in. He knew why Gaia had to disappear. But Ed. . . Ed knew nothing. All he would know was that he'd put all his trust and all his faith into someone who'd simply vanished without the slightest explanation—without a word. She'd be no better than her father. That's what it was.

That had to be what it was.

A note. She would write Ed a note and slip it under his door. Then she would disappear.

Gambling

HIDE-AND-SEEK. THAT'S WHAT THIS was. Yes, Loki's operation had been reduced to nothing more than a pitiful, simple-minded children's game. The meticulous planning, the second-guessing, the manipulations—none of it mattered now. Loki's controlled breathing was all that prevented him from slipping into a fit of rage. He had his driver cruising at a snail's pace up Hudson Street as he stared intensely through the slim opening of his polarized window, squeezing the cell phone in his tightly clenched fist. He was searching the night for signs of Gaia aboveground, waiting for a report from his men underground. But he might as well have ordered them to traipse through the subways of New York, chanting "come out, come out, wherever you are. . ." like hapless little schoolboys. It was more than just infuriating; it was humiliating. Degrading.

But of course he should have expected this pathetic state of affairs. Why should he have hoped for anything more than a child's game when he'd left his plans in the hands of children? Incompetent children like Josh Kendall and Sam Moon?

Loki knew it had been a gamble to let so much hinge on Gaia's deeply unimpressive boyfriend, and now he was relearning a lesson he thought he'd learned long ago: `Gambling is for the unintelligent and the uninspired.` One's desired outcome should always be a forgone conclusion. Now he had no choice but to sit mired in the purgatory of his black Mercedes, waiting for confirmation of Gaia's capture. And that call was long overdue.

"I'm sure they have her by now," Josh offered. He squirmed next to Loki on the plush the seat of the limo.

Loki raised his finger to his lips, cutting Josh off with a vicious glance. "*Don't speak*," he ordered. "You're not sure of a thing, you idiot."

Josh lowered his head and shut his mouth. He looked very much like a submissive dog. Which was fitting. The last thing Loki needed to hear was another presumptuous false promise from Josh. Frankly, he doubted he would let Josh live after the botched Sam Moon job. So they sat in silence as Loki continued his exercise in futility, scanning each city block with mechanical precision.

At long last, the shrill ring of the cell phone broke the tense silence. Loki flipped it open. "Yes?" he snapped, keeping his eyes glued on the passing streets.

"We lost her," a deeply agitated voice moaned through the phone. The man's voice was barely audible above the distorted rumble of a train booming in the background. "We got split up and I've been hit. I've been hit bad. I need medical assis—"

Loki crushed the phone shut. That was it. He could take no more. He hurled the sleek black plastic apparatus at a row of glass decanters on the minibar, spraying scotch and shattered glass all over Josh's chest and legs. Josh flinched, but said nothing. He began to sweep the glass from his shirt, which somehow only further infuriated Loki.

"Leave it there," he ordered.

Josh obeyed without a word. His hands fell back to

his sides. A small drop of blood trickled down his face.

"Consider it your first punishment," Loki added, sliding his window closed. He took a moment to try to regain his composure, but still could not contain himself. The frustration was like a hurricane inside him. "You *told* me you had Moon under control," he spat. "What the hell have I trained you for?"

"I had every indication that he *was* under control," Josh whined defensively. "I just wasn't expecting that kind of bravery from him. I thought the kid was a total pushover. I should have just shot him the first time he gave me attitude—"

"Enough!" Loki shouted.

"I'm sorry. . ." Josh dropped his head back down toward his lap. "At least he's out of the way now," he said quietly.

"Yes, he's out of the way, and that's another month wasted," Loki muttered. "One more useless dead body. And I'm still no closer to having Gaia. We don't have any more time now. Do you understand that?"

"I know, I'm sorry—"

"Keep your mouth shut," Loki commanded. "We'll need to use someone else to get to her now. Someone as close to her as Moon was. I have a few ideas. Do you understand what needs to happen now?" His voice deliberately dripped with condescension. "Now we'll have to initiate a full-fledged search for her with absolutely no time to work with. I need to secure her in the next twenty-four hours. That is an absolute deadline, do you understand? We'll start with the basics. Or rather, *I'll* start with the basics. I can't have you screwing things up again. I'll pay a visit to the Mosses first thing in the morning, and I will go *alone*."

Josh acquiesced with a simple nod of his head, his eyes still glued to the car floor.

Loki glanced out the window. They'd reached the last corner before the West Side Highway.

"Here!" he barked at the driver. The car lurched to a halt. He reached over Josh and yanked the door open, then leaned back in his seat. "Now get out."

Josh didn't waste any time. Shards of glass tumbled to the floor and sidewalk as he climbed from the car and walked briskly away toward the deserted meat-packing district. It wasn't long before he started running. A grim smile crossed Loki's face. Josh understood the rules. Loki had just decided to give him a break. His last.

There was a time, not too long ago, when I led by example. That was what set me apart from the other people in my peculiar field. I took care of everything—from wiring the smallest filament in an explosive to crawling for twelve hours through the muck of a Colombian jungle. I didn't place myself above any job, no matter how lowly the task at hand.

I've wasted weeks, months even, blaming the incompetence of others for my own failures. I realize now that I've become lazy. I sit in overpriced leather thrones in palatial penthouses, doling out orders like some fattened king who's never even served in an army.

That is not who I am.

From this point forward I am taking on all duties myself. Assuming full responsibility. It's the only way I can be certain my plans will reach fruition. I'm not wasting any more of my precious time giving out orders to pea-brained idiots and watching them fail at the simplest of tasks. I'll carry out my own orders. Because I have no choice. And because Gaia deserves it. She deserves better than these thugs and lackeys I've thrown at her—she's so laughably superior to those drones. She deserves a captor with a genius equal to her own. She deserves me. And I her.

She's been easy to track thus far because she hasn't known she was under surveillance, but that is all going to change now. Now that she knows I'm looking, she will be absolute hell to find. And I would expect nothing less. Which is not to say that I won't find her. I will, and I will have her on a plane to Germany by this time tomorrow night. Because I'm not about to watch years of planning go up in smoke. A few minor adjustments, and the pieces will fall back in place. Of course, there may have to be a few more casualties than I had planned. But when Gaia is the end, all means are justified.

So a children's game it is. Hide-and-seek. A chance for Gaia and me to play the kind of game we should have played years ago.

He already had an endless list of potential buyers in China, the Sudan, Afghanistan, Peru. . . anyplace on the planet where terrorism thrived.

glimpse of heaven

GAIA COULDN'T TAKE THE EXERtion anymore. She had to slow down, even if just for a minute. To catch her breath. Maybe to regain some feeling in her legs. She must have run at least two miles up the Lower East Side at full throttle, through Chinatown and Tribeca, past Little Italy—hurtling down the sidewalk, nearly knocking over several people in the process. Now she was closing in on Ed's apartment. And if she were really going to leave him a note, then it was time to stop and write it.

Words, words, words

Whatever the hell it was going to say. Not that it made any difference.

"Words, words, words."

A grim smile crossed her face as she hobbled into an all-night deli on the Bowery. That was a line from some Shakespeare play—one of many her father had forced her to read long ago. She couldn't remember which play it was. *Othello*? *Hamlet*? Whatever. She remembered loving that line, though, even then. It perfectly summed up the futility of trying to communicate anything of value. Like emotion, for instance.

She staggered down one of aisles, her shoulders brushing against the shelves of chips, cereal, and beef jerky. She squinted in the glaring fluorescent lights for any sign of pen or paper. Or at least a place to sit. *There.* Two torn chairs and a scuffed card table. Beautiful. `Like a glimpse of heaven.` She collapsed into one of the chairs, allowing her arms and head to sprawl across the rugged plastic tabletop. Her breaths were shallow and painful. Within seconds her body and mind were arguing over whether or not to give in to sleep. But her mind won out. Her mind knew she was probably still being hunted. She willed her aching head back up off the table and stumbled to the front counter.

"Can I please have a large coffee?" she asked hoarsely.

The young Korean woman behind the counter reached for a cup, then hesitated. "That's one dollar," she said. Her tone was suspicious.

Gaia blinked. Her stomach dropped. What was she thinking? She had no money. All she had was a subway card. Sam was supposed to have taken her to dinner, and then she'd planned on taking the subway straight back to the Mosses'. Now, that was an impossibility. Going back there would. . . but there was no point in rehashing the whole evening again. She didn't need the pain. She'd had plenty already.

"You go home now," the woman suddenly snapped, full of disdain. "Go on." Her eyes drifted slowly from Gaia's brown dress—skintight from all the sweat and wrapped awkwardly around her body—up to the damp mop of blond hair stuffed under the filthy black cap.

"I'm sorry," Gaia began. "I didn't—"

"Go home," the woman repeated. She flared her nostrils and wrinkled her nose to indicate that Gaia stank. Then she turned her back.

Well. So much for coffee. Gaia allowed herself a brief fantasy of leaping over the counter, shoving the woman's head into the ice machine, and pouring the stuff herself. But she could barely move. Her limbs were threatening to shut down on her completely. Besides, she knew she couldn't blame the woman for being rude. Gaia probably looked like one of a hundred disheveled, penniless kids who wandered in and out of here every day.

Go home, the woman had said.

The only problem was that home didn't exist.

Gaia shook her head. She had to maintain control. But she could feel herself slipping into a miserable tailspin. It was ironic in a way. She'd always *felt* homeless: alone, transient, without roots. But *being* homeless was something very different. She had no place to sleep, no money—just the clothes on her back. She didn't even have a warm coat. And she certainly fit the image of a homeless person: she was smelly, exhausted, and desperate. Once she dropped the note off for Ed (if she ever even wrote it), she had no idea where to go. She could hop a train at Grand Central—and stick to the bathrooms until she jumped off—but again, the same question loomed: *where* would she go? The destination made no difference.

Somehow, somewhere along the way, the thought of being alone had begun to affect her. It had begun to hurt. She couldn't just rewind her psyche to a simpler time when there were no attachments in her life whatsoever, and her only wish was to be left alone. It had something to do with Ed and Sam, and Mary. Important relationships had finally been introduced into her life, and now she wasn't sure if she could live without them. True, she'd already learned how to live without Mary. She hadn't had a choice. She was still learning how to live without Sam—to let him go. But why did she have to live without Ed? Ed had always been there, no matter how numb or depressed or bitchy she acted, no matter how dangerous the circumstances, and she couldn't say that about another soul in her life—

Stop it, she scolded herself. *Survival, remember?*

A series of images flashed through her head: the look of terror on Sam's face when he told her to run, the sinister eyes of that drunken idiot on the train. . . a man firing a bullet into his own head simply to escape the wrath of Loki. A jolt of energy shot through her. She'd already spent too much time in the deli. If Loki was tailing her, he could have caught up by now. And if he caught up, she was dead.

Don't think about what you're leaving or where you're going. Just keep moving.

"Paper," she whispered to the woman's back. "Please. I need a piece of paper. I'm sorry I don't have any money. But if you could just do me that favor, I'd really appreciate it."

After several seconds, the woman finally sighed and shuffled over to the register. She tore a scrap of receipt paper from the top of it and shoved it in Gaia's face.

Gaia forced herself to smile. "And could I trouble you for a pen?" she asked.

The woman scowled, but she pulled a pen from her shirt pocket and dropped it on the counter. Then she turned her back once more. The message was clear: *do what you have to do, and do it fast. Then get out.*

"Thanks," Gaia breathed, fighting back anger. She snatched the pen and paper and started scrawling her good-bye even before the thoughts were fully formed in her head:

Ed,

I'm saying good-bye, but not for always. There's just some stuff going on and I can't be in New York right now. But I couldn't leave without saying good-bye to you because you've been

Gaia stopped and stared at the paper. She *knew* that words didn't matter. That was the whole point.

And Ed would understand. But here she was, stuck. Her legs and feet began to shake with discomfort. No matter how loudly she screamed at herself to finish and get moving, no words seemed right.

everything

Everything? Her jaw tightened.

Everything *what?* "Everything to me?" Her breath started coming fast. Was that the sentence? *You've been everything to me?* What the hell was that? It sounded nothing like Gaia Moore. It sounded like a Hallmark card reject. A million thoughts collided in her head—all the things she knew she had to do at that moment to be safe, to keep Ed safe, and to move on. But she couldn't articulate them. Now her heart was pounding uncomfortably, and she was beginning to sweat again.

"Screw it!" she heard herself shout.

The woman behind the counter flinched.

Gaia hardly noticed. She slammed her fist on the counter and crumpled the piece of paper—unfinished sentence and all. That was the best she could do. And that was enough. She sprinted out of the deli, trying to shake every last confusing thought about Ed from her brain as the biting wind enveloped her. Funny: until that moment, she'd forgotten why she didn't make friends in the first place.

It was so she wouldn't have to lose them.

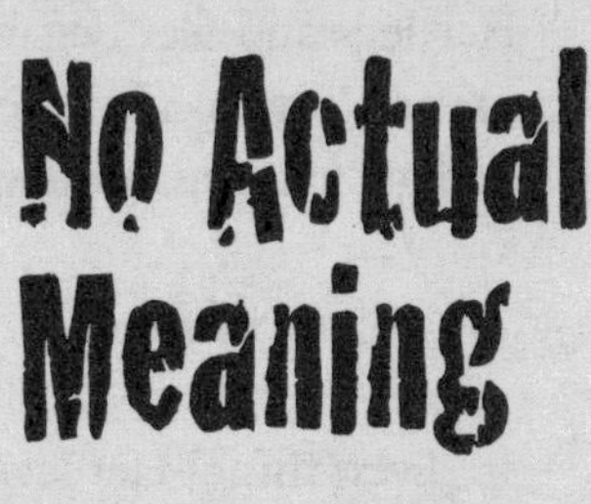

TOM MOORE AND GEORGE NIVEN FLEW through the door of George's townhouse without a word. At this point, speech was not necessary. They were of one mind now, sharing one very clear and immediate goal: *Find Gaia now.* They did not bother to flip on any lights, nor did they remove their coats. Instead, they made a simultaneous beeline for George's study—and within thirty seconds, they had begun their search. George logged on to his laptop while Tom placed a call on the secure phone line. Maybe one of the other agents had gotten a lock on Gaia, or at the very least, a more specific address for Loki's current headquarters. All Tom knew was that his twin had once again relocated in Chelsea.

"Enigma four-four-seven-Victor-Charlie," he whispered quickly and deliberately into the phone. "I need a secure line."

"Go ahead," the operator replied in a flat, inhuman tone.

"We've got a potential national security breach and Gaia Moore is out-of-pocket. Repeat, *Gaia Moore is out-of-pocket.* Requesting assistance and an international APB effective immediately." Tom spoke with clipped bureaucratic efficiency, but he could hear the uneven cracks in his own voice—the lack of breath at the end of each sentence. Panic was beginning to set in. His well-honed professional veneer was beginning to crumble. Loki had obviously been poised to put his plans for Gaia in full motion. . . at the very instant Tom lost track of her.

He had all kinds of excuses, of course. Loki had tricked him into chasing phantoms and decoys in Brussels. His flight back to New York had been delayed over and over again. But in the end, the cold truth was undeniable: Gaia was his responsibility, and he'd failed her yet again.

If she'd gone into hiding, that would be agonizing but bearable. But Sam Moon had been found dead—undoubtedly killed by Loki. Gaia had disappeared at the exact same time. Tom kept trying to ignore the obvious conclusion. It was impossible, though. If two people were together, and one of them was found dead, the odds of the other's having survived were next to nothing. In his many years with the Agency, not one missing person in such a scenario had ever been found alive.

On the other hand, this was Gaia. The rules that applied to most people did not apply to her. He clung to that idea. She was a random factor. Her fate could not be predicted with any certainty.

"Message received," the operator replied. "APB has been issued. Provide text confirmation and details online, using secure server zero-nine-nine-dash-tango."

"Understood." The line went dead and Tom collapsed on George's couch, trying to regain full control of his breath and his faculties. "Zero-nine-nine-dash-tango," he repeated to George, who wasted no time logging on to the CIA server, typing in the few details they had thus far. "Wait a minute," Tom added. "They'll want to see this. . . ."

His fingers trembling, he reached into his pocket and pulled out the CD he'd stolen from Loki's agents in Brussels. He hadn't abandoned Gaia for nothing. No, at the very least, he had returned to New York with Loki's plan for her. The entire operation, CLOFAZE, was described on the CD. *Clofaze.* The word had no actual meaning, but reading it still had the effect of twisting Tom's stomach into a painful knot.

"What is this?" George asked, slipping the disk into the computer for a download to the Agency.

"It's Loki's latest venture," Tom murmured. "It's the reason for all of this madness and bloodshed. It's my brother's notion of a family." Tom knew how absurd and melodramatic that sounded, but he also knew how his brother's mind worked. Or rather, what was left of his mind.

CLOFAZE was the reason Loki wanted Gaia so badly. He intended to use her DNA for his own nefarious purposes, first to mass-produce her genetic material, and then presumably to create an army of Gaia clones—all of which he intended to farm out to the highest international bidders. He already had an endless list of potential buyers in China, the Sudan, Afghanistan, Peru. . . anyplace on the planet where terrorism thrived. The US had its share as well.

The plan was undeniably insane, and yet it made perfect sense to Tom. He knew all too well why Loki had nurtured this ludicrous scheme for so many years. Cloning Gaia was his twisted way of finally being able to "father" his own children, or more specifically, to "father" his own *Gaia*. Loki had always wanted Tom's beloved Katia for his wife, and Gaia for his daughter. This would be the ultimate vengeance—the fulfillment of a very sick dream. Loki wouldn't have to envy Tom's Gaia any more. Now he'd have a hundred Gaias of his own. That, in Loki's mind, would be the only way to win this battle—this competitive childish game he'd been making Tom play ever since his mind had become irrevocably twisted. But it was not even enough for Loki to have a hundred Gaias of his own. First, he needed his brother's.

And now, it seemed, he very well might have her.

Tom looked over to George. "Any sign of her?" he asked.

George fixed his eyes on his computer screen with anticipation, but then dropped his head in disappointment. "Nothing yet." He bit his lip. "I'm so sorry Tom," he blurted in a breathy whisper, as if he'd been holding in the statement for hours. He stepped away from the computer and opened the wood cabinet above his desk, yanking out a bottle of Jameson whiskey and quickly pouring himself a small shot in a crystal glass. "This is my fault," he said. He downed the shot and poured another.

"Do—don't be ridiculous," Tom stammered. He forced himself to walk to George and place a firm grip on his shoulder, even though the sight of his friend's sudden drinking sent a chill through him. George rarely touched a drop, even on social occasions. "Neither one of us could have done a thing."

George avoided Tom's stare, his own eyes darting from side to side. "I don't know how our people lost her, Tom. They were some of our best. But I should have been there myself. I should have intercepted her at the Mosses'. You told me to keep her away from Moon, and I failed. She was my responsibility while you were gone. Christ, Tom, she was practically my daughter for almost a year. . . . Maybe if I'd been there myself—"

"No one could have predicted this," Tom gently interrupted. "There was no way. Even if you'd been there." But at that moment, he knew he wasn't really speaking to George. He was speaking to himself, trying to assuage his own guilt and shame. Because the truth was that by leaving Gaia unprotected, he'd practically handed her over to his sick and soulless brother. He'd fallen right into Loki's trap. His own love for his daughter had betrayed him. . . .

"But what about that kid, Sam Moon?" George mumbled anxiously. "They found his body in an alley, Tom. *Found.* No one even called an ambulance. No one was—"

"Enough," Tom snapped. He swiped the bottle from George's hands. The burst of anger took him completely by surprise, as did the forcefulness of his gesture. But George was succumbing to hysterics. It was something Tom had never seen before. Not even when George had learned he'd been betrayed by his own wife. And given the stress of the situation, his breakdown—although understandable—was extremely disturbing, to say the least.

George stared at Tom, eyes wide.

"I'm sorry," Tom added in a calmer tone. "But all this guilt and regret is poison, George. It's pure poison and there's no time for it."

For a moment, George just stood there. Then he nodded quickly, as if just awakening from a bad dream. "You're right. I. . . I don't what got ahold of me. . . ."

"Let's just move on," Tom declared, with new resolve. "We can't dwell on the past. There's no time to mourn Sam Moon's death, and you better damn well believe I'm not going to waste time speculating about Gaia's. We have to launch a full-fledged search of our own. If Gaia is out there somewhere, then we've got to get to her before Loki does. There is no other imperative. Now can you focus on that—and only that,

George? Because I'm going to need your help."

Once again, George nodded vigorously. "Absolutely," he said.

"Good." Tom placed the whiskey back in the cabinet. "I'll start at the Mosses' house first thing in the morning. Then I'll go to her school. I need you to keep working on Loki's Chelsea address."

"Consider it done," George said. He took a deep breath and sat back down in front of his computer.

In that brief instant, Tom felt a surge of what felt like confidence. But he realized a moment later that it wasn't confidence at all. It was just self-protection. It was an agent's reflexive bravado: his only shield against despair.

To: L

From: QR3

Date: March 7

File: 002

Subject: Enigma

Enigma has resurfaced in NY. Last seen at JFK, 11:41 P.M. Met by GN at 11:46. Please advise.

To: QR3

From: L

Date: March 7

File: 002

Subject: Enigma

This was expected. Continue surveillance. Provide detailed report of Enigma's wardrobe in next correspondence.

For the very
first time
in her life,
she
understood
lobotomized
what it was
to be
powerless.

"WHOA!" ED CRIED.

Disturbing

He took a moment to regain his balance, grinning at the ragged figure who'd nearly trampled him. *Speak of the devil,* he felt like saying. He'd been thinking of Gaia only moments before, as he'd hobbled on his crutches through the lobby and out into the street. Not that thinking about Gaia was unusual. Chances were that at any given time of the day, Gaia thoughts were flitting through his synapses in some form or another.

"I'm walkin' here, do you mind?" he joked.

Gaia just stared at him. She didn't answer. The words didn't even seem to register. There was no token smile, not even a roll of the eyes. . . nothing. Her lungs heaved. Then she took a step back. At that moment, Ed realized that her hand had been resting on his hip—probably to keep herself from falling over when she'd bumped into him.

"What are you doing up?" she asked flatly.

Ed frowned. That was kind of an odd greeting. Not that he should have expected anything different. First she nearly killed him, then she snapped at him without apologizing. Yup. That was pretty much par for the course. "What, did I miss my bedtime?" he asked sarcastically.

"I. . ." Gaia didn't answer. She stared down at the sidewalk, her brow tightly furrowed.

"I was taking my Thursday night walk," Ed added. "That's what I do now for kicks. Take walks. Nice hat, by the way. Was there a 'homeless' sale at Barney's?"

Gaia lifted her head. Her eyes were blazing.

"Hey." Ed swallowed, suddenly embarrassed. He must have offended her somehow. But if he *had* offended her, that was a first. "I didn't—"

"I just came to drop something off," Gaia interrupted, straining to catch her breath. She shivered, then wrapped her arms around herself. "It's not a big deal."

Ed chewed his lip. Something was very wrong here. Gaia was not herself. It wasn't the curt language, or the inexplicable rudeness, or the fact that she was obviously hiding something. That, he was used to. That was standard Gaia operating procedure. It was that she looked. . . well, for want of a better word, *weak*. And Ed was unequipped to deal with that. It wasn't just unsettling. It was terrifying.

"Jesus, you're soaking wet," he heard himself mumble. He reached out and brushed his fingers across her cheek. "What's going on?"

Gaia recoiled at his touch. Her gaze fell back to the sidewalk. "I. . . I just came to drop something off," she said again.

"Well, do you want to come up?" Ed asked, unable to conceal his concern.

"I can't, I. . . I. . ."

"What the hell is going on?" he demanded. He seized Gaia's arm and gently tugged her toward him. "Come on. You're shivering like a freaking leaf and you're soaking wet. You're coming upstairs with me right now."

"I *can't*," Gaia insisted, wrenching her arm away.

Ed shook his head. He found he was almost getting angry. "You're not leaving until you come upstairs for five minutes, dry off, and have a milkshake with me—what am I saying?" He attempted a smile. "Make it a hot chocolate."

Gaia just shook her head.

"It's *me*, Gaia," Ed snapped. "Okay? Just me. Ed Fargo. The man with the limp. Remember? You know, you don't have to say one word for the entire five minutes. I won't ask you a thing. Just let me give you one of Victoria's coats to borrow, all right?"

She sniffed.

The silence stretched between them.

"It's the best deal in town," he murmured.

Without a word, she stepped toward the glass doors.

Ed stifled a sigh of relief. *Okay*. She might be falling apart, but at least she still had some common sense. That counted for something.

He prayed it did, anyway.

GETTING INTO THIS ELEVATOR WAS

undeniably stupid. Gaia knew that. Every second she hung around put Ed's life in greater danger. But couldn't stop herself. For the very first time in her life, she understood what it was to be powerless.

The doors closed behind them.

Stupid.

Gaia could feel Ed's eyes on her pale, shivering body as the elevator clunked slowly up the shaft—and his eyes betrayed his thoughts. Ed had never had a gift for concealment. No. That was what had always set him apart from everyone else she knew, all the jerks and poseurs and Heather Gannises of the world. So in spite of her bulging muscles, she was very aware that she must have appeared vulnerable—frail, even. She absolutely refused to meet his gaze.

Of course, he was trying his best to be his usual self. Jovial Ed. Ed who always had a joke handy when Gaia's life had clearly gotten too serious.

"Don't worry about my folks," he assured her. "They're taking a long weekend with Victoria and Blane at some bed-and-breakfast or something. I told them I had too much homework—although, um, I have to admit, it was pretty tempting. Buttered scones with Blane." He clicked his tongue. "That's like nirvana."

Gaia barely even heard him. Her eyes kept darting to the elevator door. She felt like a trembling lab mouse, waiting for food pellets on the other side. Only, in this case, no reward awaited her.

"That was a joke," Ed mumbled.

"What?" Gaia finally wrenched her eyes away from the doors and turned to him. Her throat tightened. He was scared; the fear was plain on his face. He didn't deserve this. But as she stared at him, his features seemed to melt into a shifting collage of all the people she had frightened in the past. . . and worse, all the people who had lost their lives because of her, either directly or indirectly: Mary, Ella—and for all she knew, Sam. She blinked rapidly. She needed to reassure him, to give him a sign that she was all right, that she was *here.* But she couldn't lie. . . .

"Gaia?" he breathed.

"I see dead people," she heard herself whisper.

A fleeting, puzzled grin crossed Ed's face. Then he shook his head and turned away from her. It was an old joke between them, one from long ago: Gaia had done a dead-on impersonation of that kid from *The Sixth Sense* (Haley Joel Osment or whatever the hell his name was), and it had sent Ed into a fit of hysterics. She figured that saying the line now would be just enough to let him know that she was okay; she could still share a little inside humor, throw Ed a joke in return. It was just a little sign. *Gaia is still here. She's still herself.*

The only problem was that she hadn't been joking.

Tragedy

ED DECIDED IT WAS BEST NOT TO address Gaia's peculiar little remark. No, best just to get her inside and warm and dry. For now, he would take care of her body. Then he would allow himself to explore the possibility that she might be losing her mind. Because it certainly seemed as though all the weirdness and tension that had been building between them over the past few weeks was merely a preview to the main attraction: a full-fledged emotional collapse.

"First things first," he said as he opened the apartment door. "This can go in the garbage." He immediately ripped the sopping wet wool hat from her head and threw it on top of some recycling in the front hall. Then he crutched straight for the closet. Victoria had abandoned dozens of coats in there. The instant *Vogue* or some other magazine for the intellectually-challenged proclaimed an item of clothing unfashionable, Victoria set out to hide it—or in some cases, pretend she'd never even owned it. (She actually used expressions like: "Oh, those pants are *so* nineteen-ninety-nine.") But for once in his life, Ed was thankful for his sister's freakish slavery to fashion. It meant Gaia could ditch the frozen dress that was practically stuck to her skin.

"You're gonna love this stuff," he called from the closet. He rummaged though some shelves in the back and found an old college sweatshirt and sweatpants. And hey, there was even that orange furry coat that Victoria used to wear all the time—back when it had still been okay to call her Vicky. A proverbial blast from the past. She'd probably scream if she saw it now. He chuckled to himself, then slipped the clothes under his right arm and crutched his way back into the hall.

"I don't know how you're going to feel about this coat," he muttered, grinning. "It's kind of—" He broke off in mid-sentence. Gaia hadn't moved. She hadn't even closed the door behind them. She was simply standing there, staring off into space as if she'd suddenly been lobotomized. Her hands were clenched into tight fists. Ed's pulse quickened. "Look, G, you're gonna have to give me some kind of clue as to what's going on. 'Cause you're really freaking me out, all right?"

Gaia nodded. Slowly, the fingers of her right hand loosened. She was holding something: a small, tightly crumpled piece of white paper.

"I just wanted to give you this," she croaked.

"What is it?" Ed tossed the clothes on the side table and limped over to her. But when he tried to pull the paper from her hand, she kept it clamped between her fingers. Ed laughed uncomfortably. "Hey. Do you want to give it to me or not?"

"It. . . it's not. . . I mean, I don't know," she stammered. "It's nothing."

With a brisk tug, Ed freed the crumpled piece of paper from her hand. His eyes flashed over the words. He blinked. He read the note again.

The color drained from his face.

"What does this mean?" he murmured shakily. "Good-bye? What do you mean good-bye?" Ed had no idea how to respond to this. It was far more troubling even than her apparent weakness—mostly because it made no sense. It had no context. It wasn't even finished. She'd just stopped dead in the middle of writing it:. . . *because you've been everything*

That was it. No punctuation. Nothing.

Gaia shrugged.

"'Everything?'" Ed pressed. His voice rose. He couldn't help himself. If he'd been scared before, he was terrified now. "Everything *what?* I've been everything what? You didn't even finish the sentence—"

"I'm just going to go now," she interrupted quietly. Her tone was blank, unreadable. "I'm sorry."

She started to turn toward the open doorway, but

Ed's hand reflexively slammed the door shut, pinning Gaia between himself and the door, their faces only inches apart.

"Sorry for *what?*" Ed demanded, riding an incredibly thin line between anger, fear, and frustration. The note was absurd, like some cruel practical joke. So Ed ended up reacting the way he always did when faced with pain: he laughed. But the sound of it was harsh and bitter. "For the last time, what the hell is going on?"

All of a sudden, Gaia shoved her hands into Ed's chest, nearly sending him toppling to the floor. Rage took hold of him—but vanished the instant he stumbled back to his feet. Her face was wet with tears.

"You weren't even supposed to be here!" she shouted. "I don't want some ridiculous scene, Ed. I just want to *go.*"

Ed swallowed, struggling to make sense out of what she was saying—out of *any* of it. "Bu-but where? Why? I don't get it—"

"Ed, stop it," she sobbed.

"What? Stop what?" He gaped at her, completely lost. The exchange wasn't merely baffling. It was surreal. All he wanted was to gain the slightest understanding of what was happening to her—but somehow every attempt to clarify things only seemed to make her more upset and defensive. She turned her head away, trying to mask her tears. It was no use, though.

Her fighting spirit was starting to crumble. Every muscle in her body finally gave over to the act of crying. Her shoulders sagged, and her head hung forward, grazing his chest with her tousled blond hair.

"You don't understand," she cried softly to the floor, her head hanging just below his chin. "They're trying to track me down right now."

"Who?" Ed pleaded, softening his tone. His mind instantly flashed back to those thugs who'd poured out of a van and tried to jump him and Gaia in Washington Square Park. They were obviously kidnappers. And he knew they weren't after him. "Who's trying to track you down? Is it the guys from the park?"

"It's all of them," she whispered, struggling to gain control of herself. She stood up straight again and drew in a trembling breath. Her eyes were moist and bloodshot. "All the fights in the park—everywhere I go, Ed. They all work for my uncle—or maybe even my father. I don't even know."

Ed nodded. It was taking every ounce of strength he had to maintain a blank expression. With each passing moment, he grew more and more terrified. The danger that had always surrounded Gaia—the danger he'd come to take for granted, even—had never seemed more real, more palpable. He could almost touch it. "It's okay," he murmured, only because he had no idea what else to say. "It's okay. We'll figure out—"

"No, it's not okay," she hissed. "I'm not safe here. I have to leave the city tonight, or he's going to find me. He'll kill me, Ed. Is that clear enough for you? He'll kill me. He won't hesitate. I should be gone, already. I don't even know what I'm doing here." Her voice caught, and her lips began to tremble. "I came to say good-bye to you, okay, and. . . I don't know. . . ." She didn't finish.

Don't cry, he silently begged.

Every part of Ed yearned to hold her, to soothe her—to do whatever it took to make her feel safe. And judging from the way she stood there, it almost felt as if. . . well, if Ed trusted his instincts, he could have sworn she *wanted* him to take her in his arms—to hold her for a few minutes and allow her to break down completely. To be strong for her. But nobody could be strong for the all-powerful *über*-loner Gaia Moore. The tragedy was that now, she couldn't even be strong for herself.

ED'S ARM WAS AROUND GAIA'S waist even before she knew what was happening. She was too exhausted, too defeated to try to squirm away from him. But the longer his arm lingered there, the less she *wanted* it gone. She was a sinking ship, and her emotions were the drowning passengers, tugging her under the surface. At this point, she could no longer fight. She could only surrender. Almost without thinking, she wrapped her own arms around his shoulders and leaned against his chest.

"You don't have to go," Ed breathed. "You can stay here. They won't find you here. I promise."

Gaia nestled her chin in his neck, tightening her grip around his shoulders. Maybe she could pretend he was right. Maybe she could pretend to believe him. Anything was better than facing the truth. Her tears fell behind his ear.

"I'm sorry about your note," she said faintly. "I didn't know how to finish it—"

"I don't care about the note," he said. "Just don't leave." He pulled her closer to him, tightening his grip around her waist.

Gaia's hands drifted from his shoulders, clasping the back of his neck.

Somewhere in the middle of the hug, however, something changed. She couldn't put her finger on it. Her thoughts were too muddled; her mind had long since succumbed to the tidal wave of hopelessness that threatened to crush her. But it was almost as though she were trying to replace that tidal wave with Ed. Not intentionally, of course. Not even consciously. Her wet cheek was sliding back against his own smooth skin. Her lips were grazing his cheek.

Quite suddenly, her lips found his.

She didn't try to stop herself. She was kissing him. Slowly at first, and them more urgently. Every cliché for passion Gaia had ever known became a vivid reality: burning, melting, like a bolt of electric energy—

The next second, it was over: as fleeting as a dream.

Gaia didn't even know who pulled away first.

"I'm sorry," Ed gasped. His eyes were wide, his breathing labored. "I didn't—"

"No, I know," Gaia muttered. Blood rushed to her face. Her knees wobbled. *What the hell did I just do?* "I'm not. . . I mean, I didn't mean—not that I didn't mean, that was just—"

"I know," Ed muttered.

Gaia took a step back. Her head slammed against the door. She had to get out of here. Now. How could such a horrible moment be born of such a perfect one? No, no, no; that wasn't right. Her thoughts were betraying her. The moment *wasn't* perfect. There could be no perfect moment given the circumstances.

"I-I shouldn't have come over," she stammered. She could barely breathe. All the magical intensity she'd just experienced was melting away like smoke, leaving only guilt in its place. "I'm putting you in danger just by being here, Ed. I have to leave—"

"No, Gaia, please just listen," Ed begged. "Please don't go back out there tonight. *Please.* If they're looking for you, then just stay here. At least stay the night—" he shook his head, his face flushing. "I mean, not as in *stay the night,* Jesus, I just mean. . . you sleep on my bed, and I'll sleep out here on the couch."

Gaia shook her head violently. Her fingers fumbled for the doorknob. "I can't. I should be back out there getting on a train right now—"

"No!" he barked. "A train? A train to where?"

That was a good question. In fact, she'd asked it herself only minutes ago. And she still had no answer.

"Come on," he said. His eyes darted around the front hall, anywhere but in her direction. His face was still red. "You're soaking wet. You're white as a sheet. You need to *rest.* At least get yourself dry and get some sleep. We can figure out a real plan for you in the morning. Together."

Sleep. Yes. Gaia clung to the word like a life preserver. Maybe Ed was right. Because if she slept, she would be able to escape. Truly. If she ran, she would still be conscious. She would still be able to think. Right now, she needed to vanish into a black void. An abyss. Nothingness. So before Ed had a chance to open his mouth again, she darted down the hall and into his room—slamming the door behind her and collapsing onto his bed. She buried her head under his pillow, wishing as she'd never wished for anything in her life that sleep would take her instantly. But it didn't, of course. Her wishes never came true.

Especially the ones that mattered.

I watched Gaia sleep until dawn. I didn't have much of a choice, really. I sure as hell couldn't sleep myself. Maybe I dozed for twenty minutes here or there. Funny what can happen on a night in New York, isn't it? One minute, I'm taking a walk, wondering what movies I'm going to rent for the next five nights—and then the next minute, my life has changed. Completely. Forever.

The thing is, there's no way to articulate such a change without sounding like a jerk, either. It's just. . . you've never known this certain feeling, and then the next minute, *you've known it,* and now you're living a completely different life.

Does that make any sense? I might be babbling.

But I am certain of this: everything important in life boils down to that one minute. And I mean that literally. In that *one minute,* I was terrified, and then I was in some kind of paradise, and then I was wracked with guilt. And now. . .

Okay, none of this makes any sense. I need to break it down.

I'll start with the terrified part. Gaia shows up out of complete nowhere looking like hell. Clearly in deep, deep shit. Life-threatening shit. I've seen it before. I've nearly gotten killed a few times myself. The girl's life is cursed. I know it and she knows it. That's all I'm thinking as she's telling me about the trouble she's in. What can a seventeen-year-old skate rat on crutches do to save this girl from her own demented family? *Something*. I have to do something. But her enemies are real, and from what I can tell, they don't give a crap who has to die in order for them to get to Gaia.

I'm just lucky they haven't gotten to me yet.

And then came paradise. I still don't understand it. I don't understand how it happened or why it happened. Gaia is telling me I'm never going to see her again, and I'm trying to console her. And she lets me console her, and I'm holding her, and then there's just this. . . *explosion*. I don't know how to describe it. I won't even try.

The thing is, Gaia and I kissed once before. We kissed in this game of truth or dare with Mary, and that was amazing—for a minute—but this was nothing like that. This kiss was completely different. This was *real*.

See, I've only had two dreams in my young life. One was to walk again. The other was to kiss Gaia Moore. So, honestly, whether I'd like to admit or not—whether I sound like a cocky jerk whom you'd want to punch in the face (and I know I do)—my dreams have basically come true.

And that's where the guilt kicks in. Because Gaia is living in this nightmare, and my dreams are coming true. It's sick. I must be sick. I can't possibly be this worried about her and this unbelievably psyched at the same time. Can I? Isn't that what all those Greek tragedies are about? Won't the gods smite me or make me go blind or something for that?

And where did the kiss come from, anyway? That's the other worrisome part of the whole scenario. Maybe it wasn't so real, after all. Maybe it was just an extension of all the insanity in her life. Maybe it wasn't *sane.* She was so gone last night, I wonder if she'll even remember it when she wakes up.

But it doesn't really matter. Whether she has any of those kinds of feelings for me or not, it doesn't matter. Because the kiss brought two things very clearly into perspective for me.

I am completely in love with Gaia Moore. And I will do everything in my hobbling, seventeen-year-old skate-rat power to protect her.

I woke up in Ed's bed last night. I have no idea what time it was. I wasn't up for very long, probably only two minutes. At first I wasn't really sure where I was. Not that I didn't remember anything from that night. I remembered everything. But to be honest, for a second, I thought I was in the hospital. Ed's got one of those hospital-style beds with the bars on both sides—he needed them to get in and out of bed after his accident. But then I saw Ed, and I was so thankful. So relieved not to be in some cold, public place where I'd be totally vulnerable to Loki.

He told me he was going to sleep on the couch, but he lied. Instead he pulled up his desk chair right next to the bed and slept in the chair—probably for the entire night. And I felt so safe. It was quiet for a change. It was warm. I wasn't running from anything. I was just asleep in a warm clean bed, with Ed to watch over me.

Of course, it didn't take very long for reality to kick back in.

Because it struck me that I was seeing a vision of the future: me, sprawled out on a hospital bed with Ed sitting by my side, frightened for me, frightened for himself, stuck in my miserable existence with no life of his own. Someone up there was shoving this huge ugly reminder in my face.

No one can get too close to you, Gaia. Being close to you ruins people's lives.

I don't know where that kiss came from. I don't understand anything about it. I don't even know who started it. And I don't want to know. Ed's had enough pain and misery in his life already. The last thing he needs is me.

The scenario
that had kept
him awake the
entire night
in a state of

obsession

panic and
self-loathing
had now
become
reality.

Knife Wound

APPARENTLY, THESE MOSS PEOPLE were not early risers. Loki must have rung the doorbell three times already. It was nearly eight o'clock. On a Friday morning, no less. He didn't understand it. *Somebody* was home; the doorman had talked to a member of the family. Either they were extraordinarily lazy, or just plain rude. But just as Loki debated whether or not to pick the lock, he heard footsteps. The latch clicked.

"One second," a voice muttered.

The door swung open, revealing a pale and disheveled Paul Moss. He was still dressed in his pajamas.

"Good morning," Loki said with an effervescent grin. "Paul, isn't it?" He extended a hand, which the boy limply shook. "Oliver Moore, Gaia's uncle. We met right here in your apartment."

"Yeah," Paul croaked, clearing his throat. "Hi. I remember you. Is Gaia with you?" He peered over Loki's shoulder, suddenly far more awake. Loki found it impossible to believe that Gaia would have had any kind of remotely sexual encounter in the back of a cab with this scruffy non-entity. Sam Moon may have been pitiful, but this carrot-topped fool fell somewhere in the troglodyte category.

"No, I'm afraid she's not," Loki said. "But I've spoken with her on the phone."

"When?" Paul asked. He seemed concerned. "Last night? This morning?"

"Both," Loki replied.

This seemed to be a relief to Paul. He exhaled slightly.

Loki cleared his throat. Paul didn't catch the hint. Perhaps the term "troglodyte" was too much of a credit. Loki was finding it difficult to maintain a pleasant façade.

"Do you think you might invite me in?" he asked finally. He knew this portion of his search was worthless and excessively time-consuming. But he also knew that no stone could be left unturned, even the stone from under which Paul Moss had crawled.

"Oh. Yeah. Of course." Paul slapped his forehead and laughed. "Sorry. I'm just a little out of it. Come on in."

Loki laughed, too, though he failed to see any humor in the situation. He picked up the black suitcase by his side and strode straight for the living room.

"Do you want some coffee?" Paul asked, hesitating in the hallway.

"That would be lovely, thank you so much."

The moment Paul turned toward the kitchen, Loki let the ludicrous smile drop from his face. He scanned the living room for any hints of Gaia. As he'd suspected, he found none. No, she wouldn't come back here. She was too smart to endanger the lives of this family. He scowled and sank into one of the couches.

"So what did Gaia say on the phone?" Paul called. "Because she didn't even call last night and I was kind of worried—I mean, *we* were kind of worried. That's not really like her, you know?"

"Gaia didn't call you last night or this morning?" Loki asked innocently. "She promised me she'd call you when we spoke."

Paul loped back into the living room with two steaming mugs; Loki could tell by the acrid scent that the coffee was some cheap, instant, supermarket brand. Still, he smiled. The key was to keep his anger in check. This was an easy game to play. Enjoyable, even. Yes, in some ways, it was always fascinating to deal with the general populace—that vast majority of cretins like Paul ("civilians," as some in his trade liked to call them), the type of ignorant folk who could sit there and perceive Loki as merely an eccentric, well-mannered uncle. Not a terrorist who could kill Paul in a hundred different ways before he even managed one sip of that foul brew.

"No," Paul said, handing Loki a mug. "She didn't call me, but she might have called my mom—"

"*Ahhh.* Where is your mother?" Loki interrupted.

Paul hesitated. There was a flicker of something

behind his eyes. It couldn't be suspicion, though. Unless Loki had underestimated him after all.

"Mom!" Paul shouted. "Gaia's uncle's here! Are you up?"

But I haven't.

"Be right out," came the faint reply.

Paul laughed again. "She'll be out in a sec. So, why are you here?"

"Well, Gaia and I are going on a little trip to Europe," Loki said, ignoring the boy's utter lack of manners. He cautiously sniffed the coffee before sipping it, then quickly set it down on the coffee table. "I told her I'd stop by and pick up a few things." He gestured to the black suitcase to illustrate his point. "Perhaps I could take a look at her belongings. . . ."

He left the sentence hanging as Mrs. Moss swept into the room, then smiled immediately and stood. At least *she* had the decency to dress properly before greeting a guest. She was quite an attractive woman, in fact—particularly in that gray flannel pants suit. Very well put together. Except for the dark circles under her eyes. Her skin was a little pallid, as well.

"Oliver," she breathed. She shook his hand quickly and tried to smile in return, but her brow was furrowed. "Please tell me you've talked to Gaia, because I've been worried sick."

"There's no need for panic," Loki assured her in his most soothing tone. It occurred to him that she might not have slept. Perhaps she was even wearing the same outfit from the day before. "I've spoken with her by phone, but—"

"You *have?*" Mrs. Moss whispered. She closed her eyes and breathed a sigh of relief. "Excuse me, I'm sorry. It's just. . . well, thank God. She's all right, then? You know for a fact that she's all right?"

Her desperation would be amusing, were it not so abrasive—and were it not for the fact that Loki shared it himself. Clearly these people would be of no help. He could feel rage creeping up on him again. He was as much in the dark as *they* were. He had sunk to their level. It wasn't just infuriating; it was horrifying.

"I know it for a fact," he lied.

I'm so relieved; you have no idea." She spoke quickly, and her voice trembled. "We haven't heard a word. I've been an absolute wreck. I was thinking of calling the police—"

"Oh, no, there's no need for *that,*" Loki gently cut in, patting her on the shoulder. It was time to raise the stakes. "You know. . . if the truth be told. . . I feel awkward mentioning this, but I think her date with Sam Moon went better than expected."

Mrs. Moss rubbed her eyes and blinked at him. Then a look of recognition crossed her face. She frowned, blushing slightly. "Oh. I see. Well. . . oh, dear, is that why she didn't call? The girl is almost eighteen.

She can spend the night at Sam's if she wants, just as long as she calls me."

Paul suddenly hurried from the room, saying nothing.

Loki stifled a snicker. *No need to worry, Paul. You won't be having any more competition from Sam Moon.* "Well, she must have been afraid to call you," he said. "There's your explanation. Now I hope you don't mind, but I'd like to take Gaia on a little European trip."

"Oh, really?" Mrs. Moss asked, her face brightening. "How lovely! When?"

"Well, tonight, actually," he replied. "I apologize for the short notice, but a sudden extra ticket came through for me. Now, Gaia told me to pack up some of her things here and then meet her, but of course I was in such a hurry, I neglected to ask her *where* we were meeting. So, I've got my driver downstairs; I just thought I'd try a few of her favorite places. Are there any particular places you think I might find her?"

Mrs. Moss's eyes narrowed. For a moment, she stared at him, as if waiting for him to deliver a punch line to some crude joke.

Loki's smile grew strained. "Is there a problem?"

"No, no." Mrs. Moss laughed uncomfortably. "But she should be in school, don't you think?"

"Oh. Yes." Nausea gripped Loki. His legs nearly gave out beneath him. This insipid woman's question had the exact same effect as a knife wound. It was so obvious. Loki had been so consumed with anger and frustration that he'd failed to make the most simple deduction. Of course Gaia was at school. True, he knew that she'd attended sporadically in recent weeks. . . but it should still have been first on his list. And not realizing that frightened him. It *pained* him. Self-doubt and uncertainty were two weaknesses he could not afford to suffer. They had never afflicted him before.

"Are you all right?" Mrs. Moss asked.

Loki laughed lightly, his face once again a mask of politeness. "Quite. I'm sorry. Excuse me. If you don't mind, I'll just grab some of her things and be off then."

Mrs. Moss shrugged and waved toward the hall. "Be my guest. Do you think you could have her call us before you leave, though? And if it's possible, could we get an itinerary of where you'll be staying? It would just be nice. . ."

Her voice faded as Loki stomped into the bedroom, ripped open a closet door and stuffed whatever clothes he could find into the suitcase until nothing else fit. He had no time to listen to Mrs. Moss's inane requests. He had to leave. Anyway, it didn't really matter what he packed. He'd be buying her an entirely new wardrobe in Germany. *Waste of time,* he chastised himself. He snapped the suitcase shut and hurried back to the foyer.

Mrs. Moss opened the front door for him. "Well, it was nice seeing you," she murmured. "How long will she be gone? I want to be sure and—"

"Not long," Loki interrupted, stepping briskly toward the elevator. "I'll have my assistant messenger the itinerary over to your house later this morning." He paused and summoned one last smile as he punched the "down" button. "How does that sound?"

Luckily, the elevator doors opened immediately. He marched inside.

She smiled eagerly back at him. "That sounds—"

"Good-bye, Mrs. Moss."

The elevator doors closed. Loki suddenly realized he was grinding his teeth. Stress was adversely affecting him. No matter. He had one more stop to make, and then his mission would be complete. Stress would be a thing of the past.

Massive Understatement

SHE HADN'T SAID A WORD. NOT one single, solitary word. Not even a "hi." Not even a grunt. Through two cups of coffee and two bowls of Froot Loops. Of course, Ed hadn't exactly been talking up a storm himself, either.

What could he possibly say? The way he figured it,

there were two potential topics of conversation: 1) the danger she was in, and 2) the kiss. Now, under normal circumstances (or close to normal, anyway), he might make a joke to lighten the mood a little. Unfortunately, there was nothing remotely funny about either topic. Worse, if he tried to talk about the kiss, that would sound as if he didn't want to talk about the trouble she was in. Conversely, if he talked about the trouble, that would sound as if he didn't want to talk about the kiss.

Best just to shut up, then.

But he couldn't. He had to say something. *Anything* to get that kiss out in the open. Or even just out of the way—if that was all they needed to do. Her silence seemed to speak for her, though. Clearly the kiss was something she wanted to forget. An unfortunate mishap in the course of a friendship. A misunderstanding. A fluke. And most importantly, it was a distraction from the real matter at hand: Gaia's safety and her plans for the rest of her life on the lam. Surely that what was on her mind. But couldn't she say *something*? Or was she going to make Ed do the dirty work?

Yes. Yes, of course she was.

He leaned on the kitchen counter across from her, studying the color details of Froot Loops more than any rational human being should.

"Gaia?" he began. "I—"

"I'm sorry," she interrupted quietly, staring into

her bowl and shaking her head. Ed wondered what the world's record might be for the longest conversation (or lack thereof) with no eye contact. He should probably get the Guinness people on the phone.

"What do you have to be sorry for?" he murmured.

Don't say it, he pleaded silently. *Please don't say it.*

But he didn't have to worry. Because in keeping with her established pattern for the morning, she said nothing. If he wanted any words on the subject, he would have to provide them. Which meant having to eat what little remained of his ego with his breakfast and probably making an utter fool of himself. And was he prepared to do that? Yes. Absolutely.

"Don't you think we should maybe talk about—"

"You got any bread or anything?" Gaia demanded. She shot up from her stool at the counter and ripped open the refrigerator, thus hiding herself behind a solid wall of aluminum.

Ed gulped painfully. So. The message was loud and clear. The subject was banned from discussion. But maybe with good reason. Maybe there was no need to talk about it. He just was letting his own selfish obsession with Gaia cloud the far more urgent issues at hand: her safety and her future. Ergo: her life. *Gaia* was who mattered now. Not Ed. He had switch gears completely.

"Look, I don't know what happened last night, but—"

Smack! The refrigerator door slammed shut. She didn't seem to have found any bread. But for the first time all morning, she looked in his eyes. And as much as he was dying to leap across the counter and run his hands through her shampooed wet hair, and feel her fingers on the back of his neck again, and feel her mouth pressed against his, he thrust the feeling aside.

"But," he continued, "right now, your safety is the most important thing. I know there's not a lot of time. And we've got to figure out what we're going to do here—I mean, what *you're* going to do here."

Gaia shrugged, then sat back down. "I have to be out of the city by early this afternoon, at the very latest," she said. Her tone was flat, matter-of-fact—as if she were talking about going to see a concert or a baseball game instead of fleeing for her life. "Or else I'll be dead."

Ed's heart began to pound. He shivered once, involuntarily. It was pretty unbelievable—but with those last five words, that kiss had become very remote and unimportant. "So you're going to need some money," he forced himself to say. "And I guess your dad—"

"My dad can't help me," she whispered. "I told you last night, Ed. Not only has my father been gone for days, but *he* might be the one who's after me."

"Right, right," Ed quickly agreed, pressing his fists

into his eyes to wake himself up. "I'm sorry, it's just. . . hard to keep track of." *Massive understatement,* he added silently. Gaia's situation was far more twisted than any lame, inexperienced, ignorant teenage boy could possibly comprehend. Then again, *she* didn't seem to comprehend it, either. There were so many holes in his understanding, so many gaps in her history. He was way out of his depth here. And he was all she had.

Think! he commanded himself.

"Well, without my settlement money, I'm no help," he mumbled. His mind raced down one blind alley after another. "So money will be our first problem to tackle. Then we've got to figure out a place you can go."

"Yeah," Gaia agreed, slumping back down on her stool. "Someplace where I can be totally anonymous—where I can stay as long as I need, and leave within ten minutes."

"Right." Ed swallowed again. Goose bumps rose on his arms. He kept shivering, even though the kitchen was very hot. Or at least, it *felt* hot. Clearly wherever she was going, she was going alone. Ed played no part in her future. Not that he had expected to. . . but, still. The cold calculation of her voice chilled him. He shook his head. He was obsessing again. And that wasn't going to accomplish anything.

"All right, look," he said. "I think I should go to school. If they're looking for you there, and *I'm* not there—see what I'm saying? They might make a connection."

Gaia nodded, but said nothing. Her eyes were orbs of blue ice. Completely blank.

"But, Gaia," he warned, "*you've got to stay here.*" He practically shouted the last part of the sentence. His voice cracked. "You've got to promise me you won't leave this house until I can get back here and we can finish making a plan. I'll come back at lunch. I can be back here at twelve, but you've got to stay. Please tell me you'll stay—"

"I'll stay," she breathed.

It was the first bit of warmth she'd given him since the kiss. His stomach contracted. He stared at her. All he wanted was to take her hand, or her shoulder, or maybe even caress her cheek.

Which is why he turned and left for school immediately.

TOM CHECKED HIS WATCH. EIGHT-thirty. If he didn't have Gaia by five, then he'd be too late. Loki would certainly have a lock on her by then, if he didn't have one already.

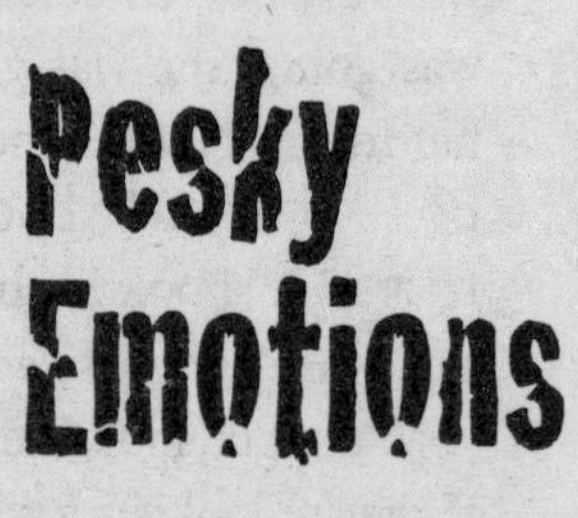

"Open up," he urged out loud. The words were muffled by his clenched jaw. He rang the doorbell again. He knew she was in there. The doorman had said, "You have a guest, Mrs. Moss." So why was it taking her so goddamn long—

Anxiety. It was killing him. So much anxiety, it was shameful. Tom knew that if there were ever a time for his consummate professionalism to kick in, it was now. Every move needed to be quick, pristine—and most importantly, relaxed—because Loki's moves would surely be so. Strange; in this way, Loki was in fact more like Gaia than Tom—less likely to be affected by the pesky emotions that clouded judgment and hampered performance. Tom was feeling all too human right now.

The door swung open.

Mrs. Moss stood before him in a gray flannel pants suit, a cordless phone to her ear. A smile came to her face. Tom opened his mouth, but she held up a finger.

"Hold on one second, Lynn," she said, covering the mouthpiece and lowering the phone. "Did you forget some of her things?" she whispered.

Tom's heart stopped. The look of recognition, the casual greeting, the question: they told him everything he needed to know.

He's already been here.

"I. . ." Tom stammered.

"Oh, Lynn, did I tell you?" Mrs. Moss chirped excitedly into the phone. "Gaia's uncle is taking her to Europe!" She motioned for Tom to come in. "I know, isn't it?...You know, I don't know. . . ." She lowered the phone again. "Where in Europe, Oliver?" she asked.

Tom clutched at the door frame. The room spun around him. Due to no fault of her own, Mrs. Moss's jovial grin had melted into a sinister leer. He could hear his own voice screaming inside his head, echoing a long list of urgent demands. *Call George now. Get out of this house and call George. Leave this place now!*

"I'm so sorry," he muttered, sliding his hands into coat pocket as if searching for something. He stepped backward, toward the elevator. "Excuse me. I'll be right back. I seem to have misplaced my. . ." He didn't even bother to finish his sentence. There was no point. This visit had yielded the information he needed; the worst possible information. The scenario that had kept him awake the entire night in a state of panic and self-loathing had now become reality. Loki had her. He had her already.

Unless Loki was bluffing.

No, that was nothing more than a mirage Tom's mind had concocted to keep him moving forward. A fictionalized morsel of hope for a starving man. But he couldn't allow himself to give up. If anything, he needed to double his efforts. He needed to cut his allotted time to find her in half.

"Are you all right?" Mrs. Moss asked, following him worriedly to the door. "Oliver, are you all right? Is Gaia all right?"

Tom punched the elevator button. He couldn't look her in the eye, much less answer her. He was so sorry. He felt a desperate need to apologize to everyone who loved Gaia: to Mrs. Moss, to George, to Sam Moon—and of course, and most especially, to Gaia's mother.

It's happening, Katia. I've lost you and now I've lost her—

Tom cut himself off midthought. The elevator doors slid open and he stepped inside. He could feel Mrs. Moss's worried eyes on him. He ignored her. He forced all the dread and self-pity from his mind, and refocused.

The moment the doors shut, his cell phone rang.

He pulled it from his inside jacket pocket. "Yes?"

"We've got a lock on the Chelsea address," George breathed.

"Stake the place out now, because I think he's got her. I think he's got her already, George."

There was a split second of silence. "I'm on my way," George said gravely. "Be strong, Tom. We've got to be—"

"I don't have a choice," Tom interrupted. "I'm going to her school to see what else I can get. He's probably been there already, too. Keep me posted."

"I will," George answered. He sounded as hopeless as Tom felt. "You, too."

She welcomed
the
sensation.
It was like
a **garbage**
taste of
something
sweet and
long
forgotten.

Illegitimate Love Child

GAIA HAD NEVER REALIZED IT before, but daytime television seemed to be deliberately programmed for people who had an intensely high threshold for boredom. Either that or serious developmental problems. These morning variety shows—all of them claimed to be "news magazines." But they all had names like "Nice Day" or "Fresh Start" or something equally unimaginative, and they all seemed to revolve around interviewing C-list celebrities or random people on the street. Finally, after she saw an interview with a dog that supposedly created works of art, she'd had enough. She jabbed the "off" button on the remote control and hurled it to the couch.

Now what?

Instinctively she stepped to the window of Ed's den, peeking through the blinds for any signs of surveillance. Nothing out of the ordinary: no loiterers or new cars. Chances were that they still had no clue where she was. She marched to the kitchen and ripped open the fridge—and then she remembered that she had already done this five times in the past hour. Still the exact same gallon of milk, container of leftover beef with broccoli, pack of American cheese slices, and a jar of olives. She slammed the door shut.

She should leave.

But no. She'd made a promise. She smacked the refrigerator door in frustration. She hated promises. Nobody ever kept the promises they made to her, so why should she be expected to be some kind of saint? She shook her head and stormed out of the kitchen to the front door.

And then she froze.

Once again, all she saw at the front door was a replay of the kiss. Then again. And again. Like some kind of broken DVD player. Where had it come from? And why had it been so goddamn—yes, it had been like this *explosion,* like every single stupid cliché she'd ever heard—but she refused indulge these memories anymore. Her mind had been playing a cruel trick on her. That was the only possible explanation. She'd desperately needed a human connection at that point, and Ed had provided it. She'd mistaken that connection for passion. She'd been weak. It wouldn't happen again.

She turned away from the door and stomped back to the couch. She flipped on the TV, then flipped it off, and then threw the remote to the side. She was acting like that polar bear with the obsessive-compulsive disorder at the Central Park Zoo. Her behavior and thought processes were exactly the same every time she got up. She'd go to the kitchen; she'd walk by the door; she'd think of the kiss; she'd think of Sam.

And then she'd feel overwhelmingly guilty.

It wasn't just that she felt guilty about just about everything pertaining to Sam—about the way she'd treated him all these months, about her inability to see what was actually happening to him, to see what Loki was doing to him. It was guilt over the way her feelings had changed for him. He'd distanced himself from her to protect her. And she, in turn, had drifted apart from him. The demise of their relationship hadn't been his fault. But the truth remained: she wasn't in love with Sam anymore. In some inexplicable way, though, she cared even *more* about him now, even if Ed had—

Stop it, she commanded herself.

And then she was pacing again. To the window and back. Next stop, the fridge.

She finally forced herself to stop at the doorway of the kitchen. This was ridiculous. Yes, she'd told Ed she would stay, but that made no sense. She was thinking objectively here. It was a bad judgment call. When the shit hit the fan, who stood a better chance against Loki and the creeps who worked for him? Ed Fargo on crutches with no martial arts training and a fully functional fear gene? Or Gaia?

Ed wouldn't even be back until twelve. This was a wasted opportunity. So. She wouldn't break her promise to him. Not technically. But she had something to take care of before noon. She would find Sam and apologize to him. And thank him. For everything. And once she had some "closure," (it was a term she'd learned this very morning from some freakish woman who owned twenty-eight cats), she'd be ready to run. All she needed was a quick disguise.

She didn't allow herself to think. She simply ran back to Ed's bedroom and snagged Victoria's furry orange coat. Then she dashed to the front hall closet. Her eyes roved over the shadowy garments, settling on a wide-brimmed sun hat and some oversized sunglasses from a stack on the side shelf. Perfect. She slipped everything on in seconds and took a peek at herself in the mirror.

It was even better than she'd expected. She looked like the illegitimate love child of Audrey Hepburn and a pimp from a rap video.

Nobody would recognize her out there. All of Loki's men would be searching for a girl in cargo pants, an army jacket, and a tank top. And Sam's dorm wasn't far. Just one quick trip. To set things straight. To make sure he would be all right. No, to make sure he got the hell out of town, too. And she'd be back with time to spare.

"ED, WAIT UP!"

Big Bad Wolf

Heather.

Ed's queasiness turned to full-fledged nausea. He hadn't realized it until now, but she hadn't crossed his mind once in the past twenty-four hours. Which was a very good thing, of course. He picked up his pace. Her voice had come from directly behind him, reverberating through the crowded first-floor hallway. He had to put as much distance between himself and that voice as possible. It was nothing personal. It was simply a crisis situation. He started booking toward the stairwell. Unfortunately, "booking" didn't mean a whole lot on crutches.

"Ed!" she cried. "Will you wait a second? Please?"

Now was one of those strange times when he actually longed for his wheelchair. He'd always been able to make quick escapes. But no matter how quickly he hobbled, he was no match for anybody with remotely functioning limbs. Heather had dashed forward and planted herself in front of him before he could even draw another breath.

"I know you don't want to talk to me," she snapped. "But I just wanted to say something to you, okay?"

She was still beautiful; there was no doubt about that. She always would be. That long brown hair. The hazel eyes. It was an unbeatable combination. So why was she so hung up on *him*? `He was scruffy and sloppy and, well...disabled.` But Heather always wanted what she couldn't have. It was the defining feature of her personality. Too bad it had taken him almost three years to figure that out.

"What?" Ed mumbled. He stared past Heather's face and gazed longingly at the stairwell. He had no desire to be vindictive towards her. But his thoughts were very far from the Village School right now. Another one of Heather's well-worded sermons on why they should get back together was not high on his list of priorities. The damage was done. She'd spoken her piece. He'd moved on.

"You tell *me* what?" Heather murmured, lowering her eyes.

"Listen, I'm a little late for MacGregor's—"

"No kidding," Heather interrupted. She flashed an increasingly rare smirk. "We've been in the same class for the entire year. . ."

Nice one. "Right." Ed choked out a fake laugh. "Do you want to walk and talk?"

Heather nodded eagerly. Ed's spirits sank even further. At this point, any kind or inviting word brought an excessively large smile to Heather's face. Maybe his choice of words had been *too* nice. In truth, he could barely maintain a conversation for more than ten seconds at a time. Everything in his life had pretty much turned to garbage: school, Heather, even the endless struggle to walk without the crutches. They were all just flat scenes from some forgettable black-and-white movie—the movie of his life before Gaia truly needed him.

"Ed Fargo walking and talking," Heather said with a grin. She must have used this line a million times in the past week. "I know you've been on your feet for a while, but it's still so *amazingly*—"

"You said it," Ed interrupted, practically diving for the stairs. Once again, fleeting pity was turning to anger. She'd had her chance to share in the elation of his recovery. And she'd done more than just blow it. She'd stomped on it, ripped it to shreds, and then drop-kicked it into the toilet.

"*Ed*," she groaned. "I'll be quick, okay?" She took an extra-large step in order to stand in Ed's way.

"Heather, come on," he pleaded. His throat was dry. "I don't want to talk about us anymore, okay? I have so many things I need to deal with right now—"

"This isn't about us," she interrupted quickly. "This is about *me*."

Ed's jaw dropped. He almost felt like slapping her. And it frightened him, because he wasn't a particularly violent guy. But after all the selfish lies she'd told him, after all the selfish lies she'd asked *him* to tell. . . how could she possibly, in good conscience, utter the phrase *this is about me*?

"What?" she said.

"You know, Heather, I don't really need to talk about *you*," he stated, his voice shaking in effort to maintain control. "I think you've got *you* pretty well covered.

There are people out there with real problems right now. Life-and-death-type problems. And—"

"But that's what I'm trying to tell you," she interrupted. "This has been a massive wake-up call for me." Every word out of her mouth seemed to come faster and faster; he could barely follow. "I realize what a completely narcissistic, self-involved, selfish *bitch* I've been for. . . I don't know, I guess forever, and I know you can never really forgive me, you know. . ." Her eyes reddened. "For that stupid, selfish dare that almost got you killed. But just hear me out. You woke me up, Ed. And I'm turning over a new leaf. I want to be selfless from now on. Totally altruistic. No more of my self-obsession bullshit. Are you listening to me?"

Ed had been doing his best to listen. He truly had. But about halfway through Heather's little monologue, he saw somebody—and Heather disappeared from his consciousness. A tall man in a black suit (a suit that looked like it cost as much as Blane's trust fund) had emerged from the school office at the opposite end of the hall. He was slowly surveying the passing crowd. *Gaia's uncle*, Ed thought in a panic. The man had those annoying, George-Clooney-style, aging-movie-star looks, but his eyes were dead, like a robot's. Ed *knew* he'd try to find her here—

"What is the matter with you?" Heather demanded.

"*Shhh*." Ed placed his fingers to his lips and gently nudged Heather toward the corner behind the trophy cases. The man was beginning to turn in their direction. But somehow, Ed couldn't move. His gaze was frozen on this. . . this vision. Death dressed in *haute couture.* The urban-chic version of the Big Bad Wolf. And even though Ed was unquestionably terrified, he still somehow felt disconnected from the reality of the situation. Maybe the stakes were just too high.

"What are you *looking* at?" Heather demanded, glancing over her shoulder.

"I. . ." Ed swallowed.

But just as terror gripped him completely, the man gave up. He turned and stalked down the hall, disappearing out the front doors—a vampire melting in a glaring shaft of sunlight.

"Ed?" Heather snapped. "Ed, are you playing some 'ignore me' game, because that is the most immature—"

"We're walking and talking," Ed interrupted in a whisper. He made a beeline for the stairs, taking each step as quickly as he could. "I'm not ignoring you. We're late, that's all." He tried to smile over his shoulder. "MacGregor isn't my biggest fan."

Heather caught up to him in less than two seconds. "What's the matter with you?" she asked, peering at him closely. "Since when have you cared about MacGregor? Okay, look." She sighed. "I know you don't want to hear anything I have to say right now. You're making that abundantly clear. But I just want you to know I'm serious, Ed. About my new leaf. I want to try to be there for other people, instead of—"

Ed stopped so short that Heather nearly tripped over one of his crutches. His body simply shut down. He couldn't speak. He couldn't move. And he didn't believe in magic powers or warlocks or any of that supernatural BS, but when he'd reached the second floor landing. . .

There the man was. Standing right smack in the middle of the hallway, having a conversation with Mr. MacGregor. The same man in the black suit. No doubt about it.

Ed staggered backward. Only Heather prevented him from falling down the stairs.

I saw him leave the building, Ed told himself. Panic took hold once more. *I saw him leave the building five freaking seconds ago.* He needed to reason this out. And quickly. A human being could not be in two places at once. He knew that Gaia's father and uncle were twins, but nobody could be *this* identical. Nobody could be a complete carbon copy of somebody else—down to the same goddamn *suit.*

"Ed, please tell me what's going on," Heather groaned.

Ed never got a chance to answer. Because at that moment, his nightmare came true. The man turned to him, his eyes widening in recognition. He glanced back at MacGregor, who nodded.

No, no, no—

"Ed?" the man called out. "Ed Fargo?"

Ed bowed his head. There was no point in trying to run, not that he could have gotten very far, anyway. No, right now there was no nothing to do but accept his inevitable fate—which was that he was a marked man. He had failed. Worst of all, he had probably already cost Gaia her life.

Cocky Mr.-Nice-Guy Act

GAIA STOOD IN SAM'S DOORWAY, breathing heavily. Until this instant, she'd been debating what to say to him first. She had no idea what he would want to hear. She'd only promised herself she'd keep it quick. That was always best. She didn't want to cry, or to argue—or worse, tell him what had happened with Ed last night. Mostly she didn't want the guilt to overwhelm her to the point where she went numb.

Unfortunately, numbness now seemed like the best possible option.

Sam's room had been an absolute pigsty before—but it had never approached this level of foulness. She took a step back, nearly gagging. Her nose wrinkled at the fetid stench of stale sweat and rotten food. It literally looked as if every kind of natural disaster had hit the room at once: hurricanes, tidal waves, tsunamis, whatever. Drawers had been pulled out of the dresser and left flipped over on the floor. Torn papers and coffee cups littered the desk. His computer was covered in dust. Every piece of clothing Sam owned lay strewn in filthy piles across the bed.

"Holy shit," she heard herself whisper.

The security guard had mentioned that he hadn't seen Sam in a while. Now Gaia was beginning to wonder just how long that "while" was. A few days? Weeks? She shook her head. In a sick way, it reminded her of the Mercer Street apartment that she had left behind—the place that was supposed to be a home for her and her father. Once he'd abandoned her again, Gaia had allowed that vast loft to turn into an indoor landfill—an unsanitary heap of junk food and clothes and dirty dishes. It was an unconscious work of art in progress, a raw expression of solitude and anger. It was the home of someone very, very alone.

Just like this room.

Sadness threatened to overpower her, but Gaia fought it back. She was on a simple, clear-cut mission: Find

Sam. But where could he go? Who could he turn to? Maybe he'd gone home to Maryland. Back to his family. That would have been the smartest move. And Sam was smart. The game was over; he'd been checkmated, and he knew it. There was nobody left for him in New York. He didn't have *her*. Mike Suarez was dead. Brendan had moved to another dorm. And then there was Josh. . . .

Gaia's blood simmered, snapping her thoughts into focus. Yes, Josh. Sam's supposed RA; obviously, he worked for Loki. That was why he'd been at the Bubble Lounge the night before. That was why Sam hated him so much, why he'd looked so tense around him. It made perfect sense. But knowing that only served to make Gaia feel more ignorant, more blind—downright stupid, in fact. How could she have missed all the clues? All that time Josh had been keeping tabs on Sam for Loki, she could have been doing something about it. Helping Sam. If he had just told her what they were doing to him—

"Gaia?"

The voice came from behind her. Gaia recognized it even before she whirled around into a fighting stance—before she caught a glimpse of that smarmy, fatuous grin and that spiky black hair.

"You must have just missed Sammy," Josh murmured.

But then his grin faltered. He frowned, giving her a once-over, examining her raised fists and bent knees.

His hands were clasped behind his back. *He* didn't seem prepared for combat. He seemed almost. . . nonchalant.

"Is there a problem?" he asked.

Gaia hesitated for a second.

He doesn't know I know, she realized. He must have not seen her the night before. He was still trying to con her with his cocky Mr.-Nice-Guy act. For all she knew, Loki was waiting just out in the hall. They probably thought they had her cornered then and there—off guard and by surprise. But they were very, very wrong.

"Gaia, are you—"

"I *know,* Josh," Gaia interrupted him coldly. "I know who you work for, and I know what you've been doing to Sam, so you can just drop it."

Josh's grin returned. Then he shrugged. "Okay," he said simply. "Have it your way." He pulled his right hand from behind his back—revealing a nine-millimeter pistol with a four-inch silencer. "This is easier, anyway. I don't have to make nice to such a ball-busting bitch. It's harder than you think."

Gaia's leg muscles tensed. Adrenaline shot through her, pumping her body with the electric, pre-combat fizz. She welcomed the sensation. It was like a taste of something sweet and long forgotten. She could kick that gun away from him and snap his neck in two before he even had a chance to exhale a dying breath.

"I wouldn't try anything," Josh added calmly.

As if on cue, the suite door came crashing open, and three burly men burst into the common room—all clad in black, all brandishing pistols. Before Gaia could make a move, the three muzzles were aimed at her head.

"You're making a big mistake," she whispered, making mental notes of the positions of all the guns.

Josh smirked. "How's that?"

"If you ever hurt Sam again, I swear—"

"Shut up, Gaia," Josh interrupted. "I can certainly promise you that I will never hurt him *again*. How's that? Now let's move."

One of the thugs stepped forward and reached for her arm.

That was all Gaia had been waiting for. As twisted as it seemed, she'd been looking forward to this moment—the moment when she could stop fighting shadows, when the real enemy presented itself. In a flash she grasped the man's wrist, twisting it back and then flipping his entire two-hundred-pound frame into one of the other meatheads. They collided with a sticky slap reminiscent of a boxer's fist against a frozen carcass—then tumbled to the floor on their backs.

"Freeze!" Josh shouted, raising his pistol.

Gaia smiled. He'd done precisely what she'd wanted him to do. Her right leg was already a blur of motion, sweeping through the air in a roundhouse kick that first snapped the gun from Josh's hand, then the remaining gun from the last thug. Still in midair, she shifted her position and aimed her heels into the respective stomachs of the downed thugs. Both connected. The two men let out a simultaneous groan. Gaia used their muscles and organs as a trampoline—springing back into the air and somersaulting past Josh and the other goon into the hall.

"Block the exit," Josh grunted. "Get her!"

She heard rapid footsteps behind her. A hand clamped down on her shoulder. Without even glancing back, she snapped her elbow into the center of her attacker's face, hearing the crack of his nose as he fell backwards and collapsed.

"Stop it, Gaia!"

Dammit. She'd hoped it was Josh's face she'd just crushed. But he was still after her—the lone attacker. She bolted into the stairwell, positioning herself just behind the door. He was right on her heels. The fizz was at a fever pitch now; her entire body was singing. Josh burst through the open doorway—

"*Hai!*"

Jump kick. Never before had Gaia funneled so much power into a single move. Her sneaker ripped a bloody gash across Josh's face, right next to his nose. Surprisingly, he didn't make a sound. His gun went tumbling down the first flight of stairs, and his body followed. He struck the wall of the landing headfirst, then crumpled. His eyes fluttered and closed.

Gaia smiled grimly. It was time to finish him off.

She hurtled down the stairs in one leap, aiming her foot straight for Josh's solar plexus. But even as she was about to strike, she realized she'd underestimated him. He'd feigned unconsciousness. The moment before she connected, he ducked out of the way. His ability to ignore pain and injury was impressive, she had to admit. Her foot crashed into the wall. She had to take a second to regain her balance. Josh was already on the attack, striking her with his fists. Loki had trained him well. That was undeniable. But Tom (Loki himself?) had trained Gaia better. She blocked each punch of his quick combination—until she found an opening and drove her knee into his gut.

"Ugh," he croaked. Blood dribbled from his mouth.

Now you're weakening, she thought.

He doubled over long enough for Gaia to clasp her hands and drive both of her elbows to the back of his neck, sending him to the floor, chin first. He groaned again. She dropped beside him and lifted his head up by the back of his hair—then smacked it back down on the landing with full force. Blood splattered on her hand. His body went limp. He had conceded the battle.

Gaia swallowed, panting. Suddenly, she felt dizzy. Purple dots swam at the edge of her vision. She knew she didn't have much time before she blacked out. Sucking in her breath, she flipped Josh over and grabbed the front of his sweatshirt with both hands.

"Where's Sam?" she gasped, sweat dripping down her face.

Josh didn't answer. He merely gave her a bloody smile—still as smug as ever, even in his battered condition. His eyes started rolling back in his head.

"Answer me!" she barked. She shook him once, then slapped his face.

"I can't," he gurgled. He coughed up some more blood. And still he smiled.

"Where is Loki?" she demanded.

"Last I heard, he was going to pay a visit to your new boyfriend," he choked out.

Gaia dropped his shirt. She gaped at him. The dizziness swelled inside her head like some kind of deafening, out-of-tune orchestra. There was only one thing that could mean. But there was no way. There was no way they could have seen the kiss. They still had no idea she'd been at Ed's house. . . but maybe they did know. Maybe they'd known the whole time and they were just toying with her. *Those bastards.* She couldn't look at Josh anymore. Without a second thought, she landed a swift blow to the pressure point between his neck and shoulder, knocking him out instantly. His torso collapsed sideways, his body sprawled out in a pool of his own blood on the stairwell.

Okay. She had to get to Ed's apartment. Now.

Now! she ordered herself.

She staggered to her feet. Her body was collapsing too fast. The purple dots turned to brown, consuming her vision. She fell to her knees beside Josh.

"No!" she groaned. "No!"

But by then, the brown had already turned to black.

"I KNOW YOU HAVE CLASS," THE man said. "I won't take up much of your time."

Ed shrugged. He tried his best to mask his fear, which was pretty much impossible, seeing how he was trembling so much that his crutches rattled against the floor. "I'm. . . I'm really late for class," he stammered, glancing at Heather. "*We're* really late for class. Maybe we could talk later?"

The man's ice-blue eyes softened. "I promise it will only take a minute," he said.

"Ed, it's *fine*," Heather moaned. "MacGregor saw you. He won't care."

Shut the hell up, Heather, Ed retorted silently. *You have no idea what's going on here. Just go to class.*

"It's about Gaia Moore," the man said. "I'm her father, and, well. . . she's missing. I'm extremely worried, as you can imagine, and I need to find her. I need to find her right away. Have you seen her?"

Heather scowled at Ed. "More Gaia drama , huh? I should have figured as much," she grumbled. "I'm going to class." She stalked down the hall and slammed the classroom door behind her.

Ed hung his head.

"Please," the man begged. "I have to—"

"I haven't seen her," Ed interrupted, but he was unable to lift his eyes. He suddenly realized a big, fat weakness in his plan to hide Gaia. He was a terrible liar.

Sure enough, her father (if this even *was* her father) frowned. His nostrils flared. Clearly he saw right through Ed's lame act. "I see," he said crossly. "Well, I know you two are extremely close. And I have to be honest with you, I'm just. . . I'm very concerned for her. I think she may be in some real danger, and if you know *anything* Ed, anything that might help me find her—"

"I really should get to class," Ed insisted. His voice quavered. If he didn't get the hell out of here soon, he might end up doing something pretty drastic. Like peeing all over himself. *Experimental surgery was less terrifying than this interrogation.* And Ed should know.

"Okay. Okay, Ed." The man searched Ed's eyes carefully before speaking again. "What's a better time for you to talk?"

Ed shuddered. Now he was stuck. If he tried to dodge all future conversations, it would be a dead giveaway that he knew something. But to arrange a meeting with a possible murderer? Wasn't that pretty much the same thing as committing suicide?

There was no easy exit, though. Ed had asked Gaia to let him help her. *He'd volunteered himself as her hero, and this was his first test.* He had to agree. Whether this man could be trusted or not, whether he was even Gaia's father or not. . . it didn't matter. Ed had to meet him. If anything, Ed could use the meeting to throw him off of Gaia's trail. Unfortunately, he might also get killed. But hey, that could always buy Gaia a little extra time, right?

Too bad he could no longer laugh at his own jokes. None of them were funny, anyway. He sighed. "Okay. I have a free period after this one. I can talk to you then. I mean. . . if Gaia's in trouble, I want to help."

The man smiled. "Thank you, Ed. Meet me in

Washington Square Park in forty-five minutes, at the fountain. I'll be waiting there. I can't thank you enough." He gave Ed a hard pat on the shoulder and disappeared down the stairs.

Ed glanced toward MacGregor's classroom. Weird: The thought of pissing off his English teacher by being late didn't really seem so important anymore. Not when MacGregor's period might very well be his last. Of course, the old Ed would have tempted death at the slightest provocation. He'd skate on any dare, and he'd take any jump. He thrived on risking intense bodily harm. It had been his primary reason for living. Until he'd actually almost died. Then he'd started to value life a lot more. For some reason, though, death just kept stalking him.

To: L

From: J

Date: March 8

File: 776244

Subject: Gaia Moore

Subject spotted at Messenger's dorm. Four-man team was dismantled. Subject eluded capture. Please advise.

To: J

From: L

Date: March 8

File: 776244

Subject: Gaia Moore

Of course the subject dismantled your team. You were all outmatched. Return to HQ. It will take far more than physical force to complete this phase of the operation. The Messenger may be gone, but the new plan is about to begin.

Never

before had

she wanted

to hurt

somebody—

anybody—

as badly as

she did

at this

moment.

no logic

TOM'S EYES ROVED OVER THE LATE-morning Washington Square crowd: the drug dealers and their clientele, the hustlers, the performers, the students and truants... all the blissfully ignorant faces in the spring sunshine. None caught his attention. But chances were that he was still under surveillance. Any one of these young men or women—these *children*—could be in Loki's employ. That was part of Loki's genius, the key to his success. He sank to new levels of depravity to keep his enemies guessing.

And now Tom had sunk to that very level himself.

Not only was *he* dragging a child into this deadly game, but the child was disabled. He'd stopped second-guessing himself, though. He'd steeled his nerves to become impervious to the implications of his actions. He'd simply stopped caring. The circumstances had necessitated it.

Loki would be proud, Tom thought. Even his own thoughts were black, devoid of emotion. *I'm becoming more like him every day.*

Tom's eyes swept the crowd again, and he immediately hopped to his feet. There the boy was, hobbling toward him from the direction of Waverly Place. Tom hurried to intercept him, then pointed to a nearby bench.

"Thank you so much for meeting me, Ed," he breathed

"It's no problem," Ed grunted. He leaned his crutches against the armrest, then plopped down beside him. "You, know, Mr. Moore, I really don't—"

"Tom. Please, call me Tom."

Ed swallowed and forced a smile, then stared at his feet.

Tom studied his face. *My God.* This boy was terrified of him. His lips were trembling. He sat still, but every muscle in his body seemed to be poised to leap away at a moment's notice. His skin was growing paler by the second. Tom felt sick. But he forced himself to speak. There was no point in prolonging the torture. For either of them.

"Now, Ed, I don't want to be impolite. But you have to understand, I have very little time to find my daughter. So if you know something, anything, you need to tell me now. Please tell me what you know."

Ed shifted in his seat. "Look, I'm really sorry. I just don't know anything—"

"I think you're lying," Tom snapped. His frustration had reached the boiling point. He knew he couldn't waste any more time. He'd have to resort to an old standby, one of the most basic methods of interrogation: using a subject's fear against him. "I think you know something. And I think you're afraid to tell me."

"No," Ed croaked, clearing his throat vigorously.

"No, I'm. . . I'm really sorry, Tom. I mean, you're scaring me here."

Good. That's good. Don't let the boy's fear soften your resolve.

"You should be scared," Tom stated point-blank. "Because if you don't know where she is, then she's probably already gone."

Ed remained silent. He shivered once, then closed his eyes.

"Talk to me!" Tom barked.

A few people glanced in their direction, then quickly looked away. Tom knew that raising his voice hadn't been a wise move. But then, he was beyond behaving wisely. Not when Gaia's life was at stake.

"Well, I know her uncle doesn't have her," Ed blurted out.

Tom's eyes widened—both with horror and hope. So Ed was aware of Loki. Which meant he must have talked to Gaia very, very recently.

"How do you know that?" Tom demanded.

Ed shook his head. "I. . . I. . ."

"This isn't a game, damn it!" Tom hissed.

"But I don't know anything," Ed insisted. His voice grew strained. He was clearly on the verge of tears. "I just know she's okay, that's all. That's all I know."

"Did she call you?"

"Maybe. I—"

"Did she tell you where she was?"

"No. No, she just said that I shouldn't worry, and that—"

"Ed, you're lying. I can tell that you're lying. You're a terrible liar." Hope began to well inside him, as did the abhorrence of himself—at how he was being forced to treat this poor boy. "You know where she is, don't you?"

Ed turned away.

Tom clamped his hand onto Ed's chin, and wrenched his head back to face him. "You're still not understanding," Tom said harshly. "*Now* is the time when you tell me everything. *Now.* Not later."

"Let me go," Ed pleaded. His eyes darted toward the crowd.

A few excruciating seconds ticked by as Tom gripped Ed's stricken face in his hand. Then he let go. This had gone on long enough. He wouldn't stoop to his twin's level. Never. No matter what the circumstances. He could always tail Ed, following at a safe distance and allowing him to take the two of them straight to Gaia—*if* Ed indeed knew where she was. Knowing Gaia, she was probably already on the move. But it was worth a shot. He reached into his coat pocket.

"No!" Ed cried, flinching. He struggled to back away from Tom—until he saw exactly what it was that Tom had pulled out.

It was a silver CD case.

Ed peered at the label, almost hyperventilating. "Clofaze?" he murmured. "What's that? I don't get it."

"Just give her the CD," Tom said quietly. "There's a note tucked inside as well. It's everything she needs to know. Tell her that there will be no more secrets. Tell her I pray she can forgive me. And tell her I love her."

"But. . ." Ed's head jerked up. He gaped at Tom.

"Tell her," Tom whispered. He didn't wait for Ed to answer. He simply thrust the CD into Ed's uncomprehending grasp and jumped from the bench, vanishing into the crowd before Ed could refuse his requests. It was time to get lost. And then to be found.

Poisonous Smoke

GAIA WAS CALLING FOR HIM EVEN before she'd slammed the front door shut.

"Ed? Ed, are you home?"

She raced through every room in the apartment, screaming his name—even though she was well aware that this behavior was totally irrational. If he'd been there, he would have answered. It was past noon. Which meant that he was missing. She was too late. Loki already had him. First Sam, now Ed. Her heart pounded. She had known this would happen. She'd predicted it.

"Ed!"

Nothing. Of course nothing. The apartment was empty. When she circled back to the front hall, she finally stopped. Her hands were bruised and aching. Her throat was raw and her limbs had become so weak that they felt detached from her body. But, as always, when fear should have been raging, her mind became a still pond. She had to rethink her strategy. At least she'd managed to escape from Josh and the others. Josh had still been passed out cold in the stairwell when she'd left him, stewing in a pool of his own blood. He'd be hurting when he regained consciousness. That gave her some pleasure—

There was a rustling at the front door.

Gaia immediately ducked down and scurried to the side of the door as the key slipped into the lock. *Ed?* Her hopes soared, but she was also poised for a more likely arrival: that of Loki himself. She raised her arms.

"Gaia?"

It *was* Ed. He stumbled into the foyer, nearly tripping over his crutches. Gaia's arms dropped to her sides. Her body sagged back against the wall. She almost felt like laughing. Well, either that or bursting into tears.

"Gaia?" Ed screamed.

"Here," she groaned faintly.

Ed whirled around. He squeezed his eyes shut for a moment, as if to make sure he wasn't hallucinating—then shook his head. Gaia nodded. She smiled shakily. There was no need to speak. She understood exactly how he felt. Without a word, he tossed his bag and crutches to the floor and shambled over to her. She put her arms around him, allowing him to use her for support. He buried his head in her shoulder, sniffling—and she suddenly realized that they were standing in the reverse of position that had led to the—*Stop it!* She thrust those thoughts aside. Ed needed comfort. She wouldn't allow the embrace to end over some misguided anxiety, over idiotic attempts to guess if he were thinking the same thing.

Ed squeezed her tightly.

Gaia felt a slight shiver, but warmth was building inside her. She didn't understand it. The sense of imminent death had become the norm—something she experienced every day, no different than hunger or thirst or fatigue. But now for some reason that feeling faded whenever she was with Ed. And it was troubling, because there was no logic to it. Their lives had never been more thoroughly screwed than at this moment. Yet still she let him hug her.

Neither of them moved a muscle. Time seemed to expand, stretching thin, like a bubble. The moment was just as fragile. They had to protect this little bubble of time, to freeze it. Yes. Logic made no difference.

Gaia was certain that they could hold everything else at bay as long as they didn't let go of each other, as long as they froze the moment for themselves. She'd promised herself there would not be another kiss. She wouldn't allow all that totally unexpected passion to rear its ugly head again. But this simple moment of silence and stillness felt even more passionate than their kiss had been. Too strong, even, for Gaia to rationalize it, or pull away from it. . . .

"I think your father is in town," Ed said quietly.

The bubble burst.

Gaia winced and pulled away from him. The sentence smacked her with the force of a bat. How did—

"And he gave me this," Ed added. He limped back to his bag and crouched beside it, pulling a CD from the side pocket of his bag. "I have no idea what this is, but your father wanted you to see it. And he wants you to read the note. He said there should be no more secrets. And that he hoped you could forgive him. And that he loves you—"

"Enough," Gaia gasped. Ed's words were like fingernails scraping against a chalkboard. Any more and Gaia was going to scream. She took two quick steps toward him and yanked the CD from his hand. Her eyes narrowed.

CLOFAZE.

Who or what the hell was Clofaze? The warmth she'd felt only seconds before melted into anger—

anger so powerful that she trembled. She flipped the case over and tore away the note that was tucked into the back cover. `These goddamn notes.` They were fast becoming her father's only means of communication. Notes that told her how much he'd loved her. How he'd missed her all the years he'd been gone. How he wanted to come back into her life. The last note had been the one he'd left at the Mercer Street apartment—a nice quick one to let her know he was abandoning her again with no explanation.

Her fingers quivered as she unfolded it.

Dearest Gaia,

I know what you must think of me. You may very well despise me. And you'd have every right to, Gaia. Every right. I pray every day that your life does not unfold as mine has. I pray you're never forced to make the kinds of inhuman decisions I've been forced to make. And I pray you never have to experience the overwhelming guilt and shame I've felt over the people I have hurt. They are all people I love, Gaia. Most of all, you.

But please believe me, I never would have left you for another moment if I'd had any choice. If it were not your safety at stake. I left you only so that I could protect you. So that I could obtain the information on this CD.

I want you to have this information. I want you

to know everything that Loki's been planning. I realize that you're not a child anymore, and that I need to stop treating you like one. I've made a terrible mistake in trying to protect you from the truth—trying to keep things from you. It hasn't protected you at all; it's only made you more vulnerable. So I promise you, there will be no more secrets.

All I can ask now is that you somehow find it in your heart to forgive me. Perhaps now, for the first time in your life, you may be starting to understand why I left you all those years ago. Maybe you're beginning to understand what it is to run from the people you love most, in order to protect them from Loki.

But, Gaia, I need you to let me help you now. Once you see the information on this CD, you'll understand the kind of danger you are in. You must let me help you. No matter how resentful you might be, no matter how much you might hate me, you need to let me protect you. Because no one can handle my brother alone. I made the mistake of believing I could long ago, and it nearly destroyed us both, Gaia. It cost us your mother.

Meet me at the Mercer Street apartment at 2:00 P.M. Please, Gaia. So you can be safe. I'll wait for you there.

I love you.
Dad

Gaia crumpled the note and hurled it to the floor.

"What does it say?" Ed asked cautiously.

"Nothing," she whispered. With all her might and concentration, she detached herself from the emotions that were creeping up on her—insidiously, like tendrils of poisonous smoke under a closed door. "It doesn't say anything."

She turned away from Ed and marched into his bedroom. If time had seemed to expand before, it was now shrinking very rapidly. She was barely aware of dropping down into Ed's desk chair and slipping the CD into his computer. Ed was suddenly behind her, leaning over her on his crutches. Gaia double-clicked on the CD icon and waited numbly through the initial whirring of the CD-ROM drive.

Once again, she was entering a nightmare. Once again, she had just finished reading a note that challenged her entire perception of all recent events. And now she was supposedly about to learn the truth of Loki's grand plan. Maybe it was just too much to handle. Or maybe she was just getting fed up. Nightmare after nightmare after. . .

Her breathing slowed.

Images appeared on the screen, cutting through the psychological smog. Cloning. This was all about cloning. DNA strands flashed before her, along with lists of statistics on the success ratio of various cloning test groups. First sheep, then chimpanzees, and finally some human subject referred to only as "the Prototype" with whom they'd had "seventy-two percent success." As quickly as that information appeared, it vanished, replaced with a list of "Qualified Replicants." She shook her head. She didn't understand any of this. *QR1: one hundred percent success, QR2: twenty-four percent success. . .* and so on. All of it popped on and off the screen with nauseating rapidity: one big blur of equations and graphs and charts.

And then she stopped breathing altogether.

The screen went blank, except for the words "Optimal Operative." And that was when Gaia's confusion and anger and nausea crossed over into something more along the lines of violent illness.

That's me.

She watched in numb shock as her as her own face filled the screen: a photograph of her profile, morphing into nothing more than a diagram—a dissected 3-D slice of her brain put on display, along with detailed descriptions of her DNA and animated illustrations of her physical skills. Another brain appeared, and then another. Gaia couldn't watch it anymore. Numbness thawed and melted into a full-blown rage. This had to be some kind of sick, sick joke—

PRELIMINARY CLIENT RESPONSE

Sandero Luminoso (Shining Path): Bid at $4 million USD (OFFER REJECTED)

Hezbollah/Islamic Jihad: Bid at $25 million USD (OFFER PENDING)

Colonel Vostok, Moscow: Bid at $45 million USD (OFFER ACCEPTED)

American Knights of the Ku Klux Klan: Bid at $2 million USD (OFFER REJECTED)

"Stop!" she heard herself scream. Her fist smashed the power button of the computer, and the images instantly disappeared, leaving nothing but a small fading dot of light in the center of the screen. She kicked herself away from Ed's desk and stumbled out of his bedroom. Ed simply stared at her. Never before had she wanted to hurt somebody—*anybody*—so badly as she did at this moment. To decimate them, pound them into the floor, step on them, and rip them apart.

Because that was exactly what her father and Loki had done to her.

"Stop it!" she howled once more. The words echoed uselessly through Ed's empty apartment. There was no stopping any of it.

To: L
From: QR3
Date: March 8
File: 002
Subject: Enigma

Subject seen in WSP speaking to boy with crutches.

To: QR3
From: L
Date: March 8
File: 002
Subject: Enigma

Assign project number and surveillance to boy. Continue Enigma's surveillance. **PRIORITY:** Collect all audio and video archives from the Messenger's surveillance. Deliver to the Canal Street Lab immediately.

I don't know who's more twisted, Loki or me.

Watching myself being dismantled piece by piece into ice-cold computer graphics—dissected into nothing more than vital statistics and strands of DNA. . . it wasn't just degrading. It was dehumanizing. Apparently, I'm neither Loki's daughter *nor* his niece. I'm his science project: a collection of genes and traits to be thrown into a magic Xerox machine so he can spit out some nice clean copies and sell them for a few million bucks. And then what? A yacht in the Caribbean? A villa in Monte Carlo? What will all that money buy? The whole thing would be really funny if it weren't real.

But the idea of being stripped of any humanity and dignity wasn't what made me so sick.

No, what made me so sick was my own reaction.

Which was this: I wasn't all that surprised.

Sure, there was the initial shock. The temper tantrum. Yeah, I may have broken a couple of things around Ed's house in a quasi-freak-out. (Okay, I guess "quasi" is a nice way of putting it.) But when it subsided, I realized that however demented the plan was, it didn't even feel all that *strange* to me—at least, strange, in the sense of being foreign. In fact, it made perfect sense.

Because I've never really felt like a person.

Yeah, that sounds melodramatic. Self-pitying, even. I admit it, even though I hate both melodrama and self-pity. But consider this: I've been watching people all my life, and they all *seem* like people. Take Heather and the FOHs in their Banana Republic sweater sets, with their Abercrombie-and-Fitch boyfriends. (Sam and Ed excepted, of course.) These are "people" in the sense that they conform to the norms of society. They worry about their grades, what their parents will say, what college they should go to, what beer they will drink once they get there. That's what "people" do, as far as I can tell.

And I've never felt remotely like one of them. Of that much I'm sure.

There was the training, for one thing. The relentless exercises in the backyard of our house in the Berkshires, the ones that honed me into a finely tuned fighting machine. There were the five years of shuffling from one foster home to another in the wake of my mother's murder. And. . . does it even need mentioning? Sure. Why the hell not? After all, it's what makes me truly profitable. A commodity. That is my lack of fear, of course.

See? I have good reason for feeling the way I always have—less like a person and more like an experiment. Like someone up there is watching me, saying: "Let's turn her life to shit, and then see what happens when we put her with a bunch of actual people. Will she be able to coordinate her clothes? Will she be able to stoop to their general intelligence level? Will she be able to go to school? Fall in love? Smile?"

You may notice that the answer to almost all of the above is *no.* And if not *no,* then at least *not very well.*

Which is my basic point. After all is said and done, I really don't seem to have developed into much of a "person"—at least not in clothes-matching or beer-drinking terms. So I really make more sense as Loki's science experiment. Because that is what I am. Project Gaia. An experiment. A failed experiment, to be more exact.

"ARE YOU ALL RIGHT?"

What a ridiculous thing to say. Ed felt like smacking himself. Of course she wasn't all right. She'd just trashed his living room. Well, maybe not *trashed*. Just shattered a few ceramic pieces of crap and pulled a few books off the shelf. He didn't care, obviously. But he had no idea how else to react. He stood on his crutches, staring at her motionless body sprawled limply on the couch.

"I'm fine," Gaia lied.

Kudos. Yes. It was a worthy answer to his own stupid question. He sat down next to her, completely clueless as to what to say or do next, or even where to look. So he stared straight ahead. His mind kept flashing back to that computer screen—to those replicating images of her cross-sectioned brain. A brain worthy of being copied and sold. And what about *his* brain? One thing was for damn sure: right now, his brain was way the hell out of its league. Tom or Loki or whoever had met him in the park should not have given Ed Fargo the responsibility of passing on this information. Gaia Moore existed in a world far beyond his understanding. He couldn't handle it. . . .

Stop feeling sorry for yourself!

Ed's jaw tightened. A silent voice was shouting from deep inside him. And he welcomed it. This situation had nothing to do with him. This had everything to do with somebody who needed a lot of help—somebody who was counting on *him* to provide it.

"I'm so sorry," he said finally, staring down at the coffee table. He'd never felt so useless in his life. He'd never felt like such an ineffectual kid. That's what it was. The gravity of Gaia's circumstances had left Ed feeling like a child whose only real skill in life was his ability to slide down a fifteen-foot banister on a skateboard. And he couldn't even do *that* anymore. (Not that it would have helped if he could.) "I had no idea he was so. . . I mean, I didn't even know they could *do* that. I read about that lamb a couple of years back, but. . . Maybe it's just bullshit. I don't. . ." He couldn't finish any thought.

Gaia shook her head slowly. "It's not bullshit," she said flatly. "It's all real. I shouldn't have let you watch. The less you know, the better."

"Don't say that," Ed insisted. "I want to know everything, Gaia. I want to know everything about you. I—"

Whoa, there.

Luckily, the voice had spoken up again. And just in the nick of time. Out of nowhere, he'd almost blurted it: the truth about his feelings for her. The three big, bad words. The words he'd promised himself he wouldn't say until this whole thing was over and Gaia was safe again. Of course, he didn't believe that such a day would actually come to pass. But he could always delude himself. He was good at that, too.

"I. . . want to help you," he finished.

"You can't help me," she replied in a monotone. "No one can help me. That's what I've been trying to tell you. When people try to help me, they get hurt."

Ed forced a phony smile. "Well, thanks for the vote of confidence," he muttered.

Gaia glared at him. "Don't take it personally," she whispered. "I said *no one*, and I meant *no one*. It wouldn't matter who tried. You don't know what Loki is capable of. And he's not going to stop until he has me, Ed. That's a fact. I need to face it."

"Come on," Ed mumbled. He tried to effect a soothing tone, but he couldn't. He was succumbing to terror again. His insides felt as if they were being liquefied. "Stop talking like that. It's not—"

"I can't let him hurt you," she interrupted, turning to look him in the eyes. "I thought he'd already gotten to you, and if he *had*, I. . . I. . ." She turned away again.

Ed blinked. Miraculously, he forgot his fear. His heart pounded. He felt his entire body constrict. Gaia had just said the magic words: *if* and *I*. But he needed to hear the rest of it. He needed to hear it now—

"You don't understand," she went on, emotion finally cracking her voice. "He can get to you, Ed. The same way he got to Sam. And I'm still not even sure if Sam is okay. I'm so worried about him, Ed."

Sam?

That was one name he hadn't been expecting to hear. He slumped back into the couch, simultaneously trying to recover from the sting of it and trying to ignore it at the same time. Gaia had every right to be worried about Sam. Sure she did. He just hadn't expected to her to bring him up at this particular moment—the moment when Ed was on the verge of confessing the truth, once and for all.

Whatever. In all honesty, Ed was a little worried about Sam himself. At the very least, he sympathized with the guy. Ed was on the verge of a breakdown after only twenty-four hours of dealing with Gaia's completely screwed-up life. He couldn't imagine what Sam must have felt like after *months* of this. He must have been a freaking basket case.

"Where *is* Sam, anyway?" Ed managed to ask.

Gaia shrugged. "I don't know. I don't even know if he's okay. I mean, you've seen what Loki can do, Ed. I just want to hear *something* from Sam before I go. Just a few words, you know?"

Ed nodded, swallowing his jealousy. "Did you call him?" he asked.

"He's not home," she replied.

"What about e-mail?" Ed asked. "Maybe he e-mailed you."

Gaia frowned. Then the faint beginnings of a smile played on her lips. "I'm such an idiot," she whispered.

"Go," Ed ordered, pointing toward his bedroom. "Use my computer. I'll. . . make us some coffee." He choked over the words, but doggedly continued. "In the kitchen. You probably want some privacy."

Gaia stared at Ed for a moment. Once again, her expression was impossible to read. Then she leaned forward and hugged him quickly. "Thank you," she breathed, a warm glow emanating from her perfect blue eyes. With that, she ripped herself away from him and headed into his bedroom.

Ed dropped his head back on the couch with a thud. He hated himself at that moment. Not so much because he knew he had no business trying to protect Gaia. He hated himself at that moment because he was wishing Sam Moon had never been born. And that was a pretty awful wish to have.

Degenerate and Evil

SITTING BACK DOWN AT THE COMPUTER was a huge mistake. Gaia's eyes kept drifting toward the CD-ROM. She shook her head. She wanted to smash it, but throwing a fit again wouldn't do anybody any good. She wasn't a moth, and that particular drive wasn't a deadly flame. No. It was just a receptacle for information. She had to ignore it. Right.

With her gaze firmly pinned to the screen, she gingerly pressed the power button, then leaned back in the chair. Every time an image from the CD popped into her mind, she shook her aching head slightly and shifted her thoughts to Sam. `It was just a matter of self-discipline.` Her martial arts training often came in handy at times like these The Go Rin No Sho provided a template for ignoring distractions: "*Anger tends to focus narrow consciousness. Allow the anger to slide through and pass over you. . . .*"

Gaia sighed and clicked on the e-mail icon. Once again, Ed had found a way to ease her mind—to make her feel as though her life was not entirely out of control. It was an illusion, to be sure, but illusions counted for a lot. Her decision to show up at his door might have been selfish, and it was undoubtedly dangerous, but it was also the only maneuver that had prevented her from falling apart completely. And Ed had pointed her in the right direction.

In all the chaos, she had failed to consider the very likely possibility that Sam had written her an e-mail. After all, a personal meeting between them was obviously too dangerous. This would be the best way to make contact.

After the usual beeps and whirrs, she was connected. And when she saw that she'd gotten one new message, her heart nearly burst with relief.

"*Yes,*" she whispered aloud. "Thank you, Sam—"

But Sam's address did not appear. Gaia cringed when she saw the ugly name that appeared instead, staring back at her in bold blue letters. She opened the message, anyway. She knew she had no choice.

From: omoore@alloymail.com
To: gaia13@alloymail.com
Time: 12:33 P.M.
Re: Are you all right?

Dearest Gaia,

This is your Uncle Oliver trying to reach you by e-mail. I'm so worried about you. I haven't heard from you since our last meeting, and I've been unable to reach you. Gaia, I've received word that Loki is back in New York City. You are in danger. You must contact me so that I can get you to safety. The time has come to make your journey abroad, for your own protection. I fear you may not be the only one in jeopardy. I think your boyfriend Sam may be in real trouble as well. Please, Gaia. Do not trust anything that Tom says or does. If you've made any contact with him, then you must understand that everything he says is a complete fabrication. That's the way Loki operates. He will stop at nothing to carry out his plan. You know this. You must call me or send an e-mail ASAP. I won't sleep until I know you're safe.

I love you,
Oliver

Gaia stared at the glowing screen. This was absurd. There was not *one* consistency, not one single truth she could cling to. No, from what she could tell, Oliver and Tom were one and the same. They were *both* degenerate and evil. Why were they doing this to her? Why were they forcing her to pick and choose the truth from the reams of crap they both threw at her? At this point, she had no choice but to hate them both equally. It was the only way she could protect herself.

But what if Oliver was telling the truth?

Then Sam was still in danger. And that was not something Gaia could live with. Not after what she'd put him through already. She had to put all her own impending emotional wreckage on hold and get a message to Sam. That was the only priority. Her fingers danced over the keys. Oliver's message disappeared, and she began composing her message to Sam.

From: gaia13@alloymail.com
To: smoon@alloymail.com
Time: 12:45 P.M.
Re: Where are you?

Sam,

I am so, so sorry for everything I've put you through. I don't even know if you should forgive me. And I wish I could thank you in person for trying to save me last night, but I don't know where you are. And I'm not sure you're totally out of danger yet, Sam. So you NEED to get in touch with me. Please. A few sentences will do, but you need to make contact. I need to know that you're okay.

-Gaia

I never realized the full extent of my failure as a father until I arrived at the Mercer Street apartment. I went there praying that Gaia would meet me. I left knowing she never would.

All my years of neglect were on stark display: in the containers of half-eaten junk food, the empty doughnut boxes, the sink filled with unwashed dishes. With the stench of rancid garbage and streaks of dirt over every surface, the apartment felt more like a cage than a home: a filthy den not fit for humans. And Gaia was the animal who had been left alone. It didn't just break my heart. It destroyed it.

I'd spent so much time teaching Gaia how to survive and how to protect herself. But it seems that she'd never learned to take *care* of herself. To eat properly. To clean up after herself. To take out the garbage. I taught her everything I know, but I left out the truly important lessons.

Those her mother could have taught her. It was my responsibility to pick up where Katia left off, and I did not.

Yet I still continue to ask for Gaia's forgiveness. What right do I have? None. But I know my daughter's heart. I know that it is big enough and noble enough to forgive me. I have to believe that. Because if she can't forgive me, then I can't protect her. Then we've both lost. She needs to understand that. But it may be too late. I may be asking for more than she can give now.

I waited for her in that hellish apartment for an hour. With George already staking out the Chelsea loft, I finally left with no other choice but to stake out Ed's building and wait. Wait for Loki to make a move. Wait for Gaia to appear. I'd never imagined it could get this bad. If my brother's goal was to rob me of all the love in my life, then it seems he has finally succeeded. I wish I could tell him that. Maybe if he knew, he'd put a stop to all this.

Maybe I should stop lying to myself.

Maybe he was
already dead,
and this was the
afterlife—a
freakish
dream world where
everybody
morphed into
the person they
always should
have been.

wave of fury

"PLEASE. . . HELP. . . ME. . . Gaia. . . Gaia."

The sound of Sam Moon's voice provided Loki with a surprising, almost childlike pleasure. He felt renewed confidence. It was a sweet breath of relief amidst the string of failures this travesty of an operation had become, and all the more pleasant because he'd expected the task to be drudgery. But advances in technology—whether audio, scientific, or military—never ceased to thrill him. Nobody but Loki truly understood how the exploitation of technological advancement was the key to power. Well, except men like Bill Gates, perhaps. But Loki had taken that philosophy to a far more sublime level.

"Again," he commanded, tempering his smile. "Let me hear it again."

The high-pitched squeal of a voice on rewind echoed through the windowless Canal Street sound studio. The engineer's gnarled fingers deftly made adjustments on the computer's mixing program. Then he pressed "play." Once again, Sam Moon's voice echoed through the massive black speakers hanging down from all four walls.

"So. . . sorry. . . Gaia."

Loki frowned. The words sounded stilted and

much too far apart. But before he could open his mouth, the engineer clicked his mouth and turned a few of the faders on the massive soundboard.

"I'm so sorry, Gaia."

Ah, perfect, Loki thought. Smooth as silk. Completely organic. As if Moon were sitting in the room with them, begging Loki for his life. All those hours of visual and audio surveillance were finally paying off. And even though the plans had nearly been ruined, Loki was almost glad he had been forced to change them. The new plan was so superior: the kind of irresistible psychological snare that would lure even the most strong-willed human being out of hiding. It was pure, a sterile dagger to cut straight to Gaia's heart. And then Loki would take that heart and make it his own.

"Let's just hear that last part again," Loki requested. He almost felt like rewarding this fat, bearded slob in some way. The man had far exceeded his expectations—both in professionalism and speed.

"*. . . please,*" Sam was murmuring.

"Hmm," Loki mused. He leaned back in the plush leather chair. "We must have a better 'please.' Something a little more pathetic. . ."

The engineer scrolled through a list of audio files on the computer, then clicked the mouse again.

"*Please!*" Sam's voice was suddenly urgent, whiny. Groveling.

"That's the one," Loki said, nodding with satisfaction. "Upload and attach it. I have to thank you. You truly lived up to your reputation."

"Thank you sir," the engineer replied humbly, turning to the computer.

Loki reached for the revolver in his suit jacket. But then he hesitated. Instead, he patted the engineer on the back. Yes, he might even have to make this man a full-time employee. He could actually deliver on a promise—a trait that was becoming increasingly rare among the clods who worked for him. To kill him now would be a needless waste. And Loki had wasted plenty already. Better to invest in skill than ensure silence.

On a case-by-case basis, of course.

A Taste

GAIA STARED DOWN AT THE STREET from Ed's bedroom window. A bitter taste rose in her throat as her eyes zeroed in on three black sedans parked outside the apartment.

"That one. . . that one, and that one," she said coldly, pointing them out. "They're staking the place out."

"How do you know?" Ed whispered over her shoulder.

"I just know," Gaia replied matter-of-factly. Yes, it was another useless skill passed on to her by her father: the ability to spot vehicles that didn't quite fit. "They think you'll lead them to me. If they don't already know I'm here."

"I don't understand," Ed said. "How could they—"

"My father led them to you," she interrupted. Her gaze remained fixed to the tinted windows of the car in front. "Thanks, Dad," she added, with bitter sarcasm. "They might even work for him. I don't really give a shit anymore."

Ed tapped her lightly on the arm. "Gaia? Can you come back, please? You sound like a robot and it's freaking me out. Do *not* give up here, okay? We'll figure something out, I swear."

Gaia didn't bother to reply. She knew that if she did, she'd only freak Ed out even more. Because there was no way they could possibly figure something out. They were trapped. Ambushed. Anybody with even the slightest knowledge of military tactics or history knew that ninety-nine out of a hundred ambushes ended in death for the ambushed. So there really was no point in trying to plot a daring escape. She could almost hear her own pulse slowing down. Her spirits were flatlining. She'd given up.

"What about the service entrance?" Ed asked, sounding hopeful. Well, either hopeful or just plain desperate. "It leads to an alley out back that'll take us right to First Avenue."

She shook her head. "That would be the first place they would expect. There are guys stationed there already. I'm sure of it."

"Okay, okay," Ed replied, "but there has to be—"

A melodic *ding-dong* from the computer cut him off.

"What was that?" Gaia asked, glancing at the screen. It sounded like a doorbell.

"I got an e-mail," Ed mumbled. His eyes remained grimly and firmly fixed to the street below. "It's nothing. Ignore it. It's probably my parents, writing to tell me that they're going horseback riding with Blane or something. . . ."

But Gaia couldn't ignore it. A realization struck her: She'd forgotten to log off. Which meant the message was for *her*.

"Sam," she murmured out loud. Quick as a flash, she bolted to the desk chair. Her eyes widened. *Yes!* She clicked on the new e-mail—and when she saw the author's name on the screen, it was a shot of pure adrenaline, kick-starting her heart. *Sam wrote back.* Which meant he was okay. The one concern that had been haunting her since the morning could finally be put to rest. A shaky sigh escaped her lips. Now she could refocus. Now she could move on.

She clicked open the message.

From: smoon@alloymail.com

To: gaia13@alloymail.com

Time: 3:45 P.M.

Re: Where are you?

Hello, Gaia. This is not Sam. But there is a message from Sam attached.

WARNING: The attached file contains a scene of a violent and upsetting nature. You will undoubtedly find the contents objectionable.

All apologies.

Attachment: poorSam.mpg

Gaia bit her lip. Relief was instantly replaced by pain. It rose like smoke into her chest. So. The message was from Loki. Sam was not okay. He was not safe. And she did not want to see the attached file. Her mind had already begun to concoct endless scenes of what might appear on screen: a hanging, a lethal injection, an electrocution. But, as always, fearlessness won out.

She clicked on the attachment. A video clip began to play.

For the first few moments, the screen was black. And then she heard his voice.

Sam's voice. It sounded strained and short of breath. Pained, almost.

"Gaia. . . ? Gaia. . . I don't know if you can hear me. . ."

She fought the wave of fury building inside her. She had to stay calm enough to let the message finish. But there was something so strange about the way he spoke. . . Gaia couldn't put her finger on it. She'd never heard him sound so *soulless*—so cold and removed. Not even all those months ago, when he'd been kidnapped the first time, when she'd received a video much like this one. They must have tortured him.

"I'm so sorry, Gaia," he said. "But I'm in real trouble here. Real trouble."

And then an image faded into view: a stark, low-resolution clip—extremely grainy. Every movement looked more like a jumpy series of stills than a moving picture. But it was clear enough. Clear enough to make Ed gasp slightly from behind the chair. Clear enough to make Gaia cringe.

It was Sam's face.

Agony was etched into every feature, as if with a knife. In the middle of his forehead, perfectly dead center, was a bright red light no larger than a dime. A beam from a laser gun sight. Gaia held her breath. She knew there was a very distinct possibility that she was about to see Sam Moon executed on low-grade digital videotape—shot in the head in full close-up. . . and she didn't even blink. Where the fear should have been, there was nothing but focused rage, tingling energy.

The camera began to pull out. Gaia saw that she Sam's face was being filmed through a window. That was why the quality of the image was so poor. Whoever was responsible for the footage must have been standing outside the building where Sam was being held—or maybe in a building across the street. And there was someone behind Sam, as well. *Josh.* Gaia's breathing quickened. Her hands clenched into fists. The son of a bitch had Sam's arms pinned behind his back. With his free hand, Josh gripped the back of Sam's neck—forcing him to stare straight into the barrel of the unseen gun that was trained on his skull.

This is videotape, Gaia reminded herself. *These events have already taken place.* She could not step into the screen and crack Josh's skull. She could not sprint to wherever the hell Sam was and break the door down.

All she could do was watch.

"They just want to talk to you, Gaia," Sam croaked in that haunting, inhuman voice. "They just want you to come to them. And then they'll let me out of this. . . ."

Gaia's fists trembled. Images of what she would do to Josh flooded her brain. She should have killed him when she had the chance. It had been dumb to leave him in the stairwell like that. Childish. Striking him from the face of the earth wouldn't have troubled her conscience. Not for an instant. She swore to herself she wouldn't make that mistake again. She couldn't live with the regret.

"I'm so sorry," Sam continued. "I thought I was out of this, but I was wrong. I need you. Please help me, Gaia. *Please.*"

Again, Gaia cringed. That last word. . . it stung more than anything else in the message. The sound was so hopeless. So scared. So unlike she'd ever heard him before. For one very brief moment, her throat tightened, and tears began to well in her eyes. But then the anger rushed back with twice the intensity. It was like a magical healing potion throughout her entire body. She would help him. Oh, yes. She would help him and herself in the process.

The video faded to black. A series of short sentences flashed on the screen.

DÉJÀ VU, ISN'T IT?
YOU WANT HIM AND WE WANT YOU.
LET'S MAKE A TRADE.
410 WEST 27TH STREET. APARTMENT #53.
SEE YOU SOON.

And then it was over. No more excruciating footage to witness. No more desperate pleas to hear. Ed's room filled with silence. Gaia nodded. The emotion was gone. All that was left inside her now was a sharp new clarity of mind. That gnawing feeling of helplessness and immobility fell away like a layer of dead skin, and she was alive again—inspired by a couple of simple truths and a clear purpose.

She couldn't hide anymore. The time for hiding was over. She had to get out of there and free Sam. She might have had a hundred questions about her own life, but saving Sam's came first. If Loki really wanted her so badly, then he could have her. She would come to him. She would get just as close as he wanted. Because it was time *he* got a taste of what happened to people who got too close to Gaia Moore.

The Warm Fuzzies

ED NOW KNEW WHAT IT FELT LIKE to drown.

It was true. He wasn't feeling sorry for himself, or trying to be poetic. He didn't go for that BS. He truly *was* drowning. The ocean of Gaia's horrors had swallowed him. He couldn't see the surface anymore. He wasn't even sure which way was up and which was down. He only knew that he couldn't breathe, that panic was no longer something he could control. A dull, red haze filled his brain.

Once the video clip had ended, he stood stock

still. He couldn't bring himself to look at her. His thoughts drifted back to the resentment he'd felt for Sam, anger that Sam was even an object of Gaia's concern. It was so pitiful. So shameful. This wasn't about who Gaia loved more. This was about life and death. `Well, at this point, pretty much just death.` They were all drowning: Sam, Gaia, Ed. . . maybe even others. Staying alive wasn't just a tenuous proposition, it was pretty much an impossibility.

"Hey. . . hey, Gaia," Ed stammered. "I'm starting to think that maybe we should call the cops or something—"

"And tell them what?" she snapped. She whirled around with a strange new resolve in her eyes. Her robotic tone had been replaced by something much stronger, though just as cold. He took a step back. Reality was losing its grip on the two of them; he could feel it. "Calling the cops will get Sam killed. Period. I just have to go there and face Loki. And once I face him, you'll all be free from this bullshit. From my curse. Nobody deserves this. Even *I* don't deserve this. But I have to deal with it."

Ed blinked. "Gaia, please don't be a martyr. You're not—"

"I'm not being a martyr, Ed," she barked angrily. "I'm just doing what I should have done in the first place. I'm not going to let your life be affected by this.

I'm not going put you in danger, like I did Sam. And you *are* in danger, Ed. I'm sure they traced that download and are on their way up here right now. That's how Loki operates: quick and to the point. And when he comes, I'm going to go with him."

Ed shook his head. He opened his mouth, but no words would come.

"We're out of options, Ed," she stated. "Not that we ever had any options to begin with—"

Pounding at the door silenced her.

Blood drained from Ed's face. The noise filled the apartment: hard and insistent. Ed looked at Gaia. Their gazes locked. She shrugged, as if to say: *What did I tell you?* He turned toward the bedroom door. How could she be so freaking calm? He experienced a quick irrational hope that maybe whoever was on the other side of the door would just go away. Maybe the pounding would simply stop. But it didn't. It grew louder, quicker. Like his own goddamned pulse. Maybe he would just have a heart attack before anything happened. There were worse ways to go.

"I'll get it," Gaia whispered, pushing herself from the chair.

"No way." He found himself planting his body firmly between Gaia and the door. He felt as if he were watching somebody else: a much less cowardly (and probably much more idiotic) version of Ed Fargo. "I'll get it. They still don't know you're here for sure. I can get rid of them."

Gaia folded her arms across her chest. "I want to deal with this now."

Well, there was no point in arguing. It was decision time. He flung out an arm and shoved her back into the chair, then spun and crutched out into the hall, striding for the front door as quickly as possible.

"Jesus, Ed—"

"Shhh!" he hissed.

Miraculously, she didn't follow. Not that this was any kind of triumph. The booming knocks echoed toward him. He was beginning to lose all the feeling in his face and hands. The door loomed before him, rattling in its hinges. Ed forced himself to take that last crucial step. He drew in his breath. If they shot him, Gaia would hear it—and then she could make an escape. He could buy her some time. It wasn't a possibility that filled him with the warm fuzzies, but it was all he had. So. Time to make a move. His life hadn't been a *total* waste. Better to go out a hero than a chump. Or, at least, a little of both. He peered through the peephole.

What the—

There, in the fish-eye glass, was a distorted Heather Gannis. Her face was twisted in an ugly scowl. She slammed her fist into the door again.

Ed exhaled, shaking off his dizziness. Well, today

was certainly a day of exploring new emotional territory. In this case, it was a bizarre and extreme mix of relief and annoyance. Not an enjoyable combo. Was it his imagination, or had Heather chosen today of all days to become his stalker? Didn't she know that harassment was against the law? And talk about a disappointment. He couldn't believe he'd practically watched his whole life flash before his eyes because *she* was at the door.

"Ed!" she barked, her voice muffled.

"Chill out," he groaned. He unlatched the door and swung it open. "Why don't you just get yourself a battering ram?"

"I prefer the axe," she mumbled, stepping into Ed's apartment uninvited. "Now, do you want to tell me what the hell is going on with you?"

"Why don't you come in?" Ed asked sarcastically. He slammed the door shut.

"Stop avoiding the question, Ed."

"I'm sorry, do you know what trespassing is?"

"Just tell me what is going on with Gaia and her father, all right? Why didn't you come back to school?"

Ed stared at her in disbelief. "Heather. Why aren't *you* at school right now? Actually, wait. Don't answer. Just leave. Because I think it is safe to say that this is the last possible thing I can deal with right now—"

"Ed, don't patronize me," she grumbled, heading for the living room. "I hate it when you patronize me.

I'm not leaving until I understand what is happening here."

Ed shot a quick glance back down the hall. "Don't piss me off right now," he warned. "I'm trying to be nice. A lot nicer than you deserve."

Heather whirled and glared at him. "Thanks. That makes me feel wonderful."

"I don't really care, all right?" Ed shouted, exasperated. "I don't know what else to say to you. Now get the hell out!"

"I want to know what's going *on*," she whined.

For the second time in his life (and in the same day, ironically), Ed felt like punching her in the face. "Why?" he spat.

"Because I want to help," Heather muttered, lowering her eyes.

His jaw dropped. His anger suddenly evaporated. *Whoa.* That was about the last thing he would have expected Heather Gannis to say. He wasn't even aware the word "help" was part of her vocabulary.

"I've been trying to tell you, Ed," she went on. "I don't want to be a selfish bitch anymore. My selfishness has totally screwed up your life. I want to make it up to you. I want to do something for *you*. If something is wrong, will you just let me help you if I can? Please? What can I do to help?"

As was becoming the norm, Ed found that he was

speechless. Incredible. Heather really *was* trying to change. The problem was, she couldn't have picked a worse time to do it. What could *anybody* do to help? No matter how sincere Heather's question might have been, the answer was still a resounding *nothing*. There was nothing anybody could do. If Heather wanted to help, she should just save herself and not get involved. Otherwise, she would just add to the body count.

"Ed?" she prodded.

"Nothing, Heather," he murmured. He shook his head. "I'm sorry—"

"I think maybe there is."

Ed flinched. Gaia was standing at the entrance of the hallway. He hadn't even heard her emerge from the bedroom. Ed's eyes flashed from Gaia to Heather, watching as Heather's face shriveled with resentment. *Uh-oh.* He could feel a catfight coming on. Just what they needed.

"What are *you* doing here?" Heather demanded. "Aren't you supposed to be missing or something? Or do you just live here now?"

"She's in real trouble," Ed piped up before Gaia could answer. "And so is Sam. And I'm trying to help. And if you're serious about this 'new leaf' you're turning over, if you really want to do something for me, then you'll do something for *her*." The words tumbled out in a rush. But he had to say them.

Heather's lips tightened. The seconds ticked by in

silence as she stared at Ed. There was no way she would ever stick around. Not now. Not when she knew who was involved. But that was fine with him. She didn't deserve to get hurt anymore than they did.

He didn't get it, though. She wasn't budging.

Slowly, her features relaxed. Her gaze shifted back to Gaia.

"What can I do?" she asked simply.

Ed gasped. Of all the unbelievable things he'd witnessed today, in a way, this was the most far-fetched. Heather's offering to help Gaia? Maybe there *had* been an assassin at the door. Maybe he was already dead, and this was the afterlife—a freakish dream world where everybody morphed into the person they always should have been.

Gaia just smiled. "I have a plan. But we're going to need the FOHs."

Heather grimaced. "The *whats?*"

"Your friends. The Friends of Heather. We'll need them now. All of them."

To: L

From: J

Date: March 8

File: 776244

Subject: Gaia Moore

Download of file was completed. ISP trace confirms Ed Fargo's ISP address. The subject is in that building.

To: J

From: L

Date: March 8

File: 776244

Subject: Gaia Moore

Confirmed. Proceed as planned.

The secret
that had
been
festering
inside him
was

clones

finally out,
whether it
meant
anything to
her or not.

IT WAS AN IMAGE GAIA HAD ONLY seen in horrid fantasies: an all-star team of perfectly-primped FOHs, standing in a kind of pyramid formation in the hallway outside Ed's door. Heather was in front, flanked on one side by Carrie and Megan, on the other by Melanie and Laura. Each girl held a plastic shopping bag in her hands, and they were staring down Gaia with a look she could not even begin to decipher. They'd gazed at her with pure disgust so many times before—scanning her daily wardrobe from top to bottom, whispering hare-brained insults that were inevitably followed by piercing high-pitched giggles. But now they were silent. What were they even thinking?

Frightening

"Well, we're here," Heather said. She didn't sound very happy.

Instinct screamed at Gaia to slam the door in their faces, but she knew that this instinct was the foundation for the subtle beauty of this plan. If Loki had been watching Gaia as carefully as he seemed to have been, then he knew full well that she had no female friends. He would never suspect the help of girls. Never.

"Come on in," Gaia said, stepping aside.

Without a word, they marched in single file—all of them eyeing Gaia curiously as they passed. She had no idea how Heather had managed to do it. . . but Gaia really had to take her hat off to the girl. Unless they'd taken practical jokes and cruelty to a new low, it seemed as though they were committed. Why else would they have come? It was nothing short of a miracle.

"Where should we change?" Carrie asked. She didn't sound snobbish or bored, as per usual. In fact, she sounded eager.

"Follow me," Ed said. He led them to his bedroom.

Heather must have told them some lie, Gaia realized, watching them leave. She and Heather were left standing alone in the front hall. *She must have told them that something glamorous or exciting was going to happen. Then again, she doesn't know much of the truth herself.*

Heather glanced at her, then quickly looked away.

"Why are you doing this?" Gaia suddenly demanded. The question was meant to sound grateful, but there was a harsh undertone to her words. The bitterness was too deeply ingrained. Months of resentment were hard to erase, even under these circumstances.

"Because Ed asked me to," Heather answered. She paused for a moment, then looked Gaia straight in the eye. "And because I'm sick of myself. It's time to flush my past down the toilet. Especially the painful stuff. You know?"

Gaia nodded. Her heart contracteed with guilt. She couldn't help but wonder if "the painful stuff" was a veiled reference to that lonely fall night all those months ago, when Gaia had allowed Heather to wander into Washington Square Park—right into the arms of an attacker. Perhaps Heather was forgiving her for that. Or perhaps Heather was asking for Gaia's forgiveness for all the shit she'd put her though. Either way, Gaia glimpsed something in that moment: a warmth in Heather's eyes she'd never realized existed. For the first time in her entire life, she thought she could understand why Sam and Ed had both fallen for her. But now was not the time for some corny confession.

"Why are your friends doing it?" Gaia asked.

"Because I told them to," Heather said, and her tone was cold again. "If you want to know the truth, I've been falling out of touch with them a little. This is a good excuse to get back in the loop. That's all." She hesitated, smirking. "And because they're all secretly dying to look like you."

Gaia's eyes narrowed. That statement wasn't just bizarre; it was offensive. Those girls had been ripping her to shreds for almost a year. Heather was obviously making fun of her. So much for the warmth. Whatever. People didn't become angels overnight. Gaia included. Heather could be allowed a couple of cheap shots. This was hard enough for both of them. Gaia would let it pass.

Heather sighed. "I'm going to go change. Here are your clothes." She handed Gaia a shopping bag, then vanished down the hall. "You can pay me back whenever."

Gaia nodded. Yes. She would be sure to pay Heather back for this, and very soon. Not just for the expense. She owed Heather more than she could even articulate. Which would be terribly frightening in its own right—if she had any clue was to what "frightening" meant.

Twins

HEATHER GAPED AT HER REFLECTION in Ed's mirror. She wasn't sure what she was going through. Maybe it was horror. Definitely confusion. Her body tingled with an extremely unpleasant, prickly sensation—as if she'd just been poked with thousands of ice-cold needles. And then she realized what it was. She was giving herself the creeps. Which was very fitting.

So this is what it feels like. This is what it feels like to be Gaia Moore.

Her fingers trembled slightly as she ran her hand through the long blond wig she'd just put on. Then she tugged on the tank top and army pants she'd bought at the army-navy store on Bleecker. She grinned. Pretty damn close, she had to admit. Except for the eyes. And face. Besides, Heather knew she couldn't begin to understand what it *really* felt like to be Gaia. Nor did she care to, quite frankly. But dressing in this freakish way was, well. . . *empowering.* She could almost imagine what was like not to give a shit about anything or anyone.

Almost.

Heather leaned forward toward the mirror. Her lips curled in an approximation of that disinterested sneer Gaia always seemed to affect at school. Now *that* was power. She almost laughed. What would it be like to beat a bunch of testosterone-soaked jocks to a pulp the next time they leered at her? It must feel pretty damn good—

"Heather?" There was knock on the door. It was Gaia.

"One sec!" Blood rushed to Heather's face. She straightened and dropped the sneer. *Jesus.* What if Gaia had seen that little display? She wouldn't have been able to explain it. She barely knew what it meant herself.

The door opened, and Gaia stepped silently into the bathroom.

Heather gave her a quick glance from head to toe. The prickly sensation returned. They were twins. The hair, the tank top, the army pants. . . all of it matched perfectly. Their gazes met for a moment, then shifted to the mirror at the exact same time.

There was no telling them apart—at least, not for a few seconds.

"Holy shit," Gaia breathed, as if she'd just discovered a particularly disgusting alien life form. "Look at us. What's the world coming to?"

"Good question," Heather muttered. She didn't really want to answer it, either. But now that Gaia was standing right beside her, she noticed that their faces were actually more alike than she'd previously suspected. Their cheekbones were similar: high and defined. As were their small noses. Only the eyes truly gave Heather's identity away.

Gaia grabbed a comb from the side of the sink and began carefully flattening her hair to better match the wig.

"Look, I'm sorry I let you walk into the park that night," she abruptly announced.

Heather turned with a start. Where the hell had *that* come from? But Gaia just kept combing her hair, as if she had merely commented on the weather or something equally as stupid. Apparently, the thought had just popped into her head. Unfortunately, it produced some very sudden, and very horrifying flashbacks for Heather. The glimmer of a blade. The searing pain as the knife punctured her body.

She shivered with the memory. Anger crept up on her. The wounds may have healed, but the scars remained. Particularly the mental ones. Why *had* Gaia let her walk into the park that night, knowing there were skinheads in there with knives? She'd warned some of Heather's friends to steer clear of the park. But she hadn't bothered to warn Heather. So either Gaia hated her that much, or cared that little.

"I never meant for that night to go down like that," Gaia said quietly, as if answering an unspoken accusation. She placed the comb back on the sink counter and turned to Heather. "It was a total misunderstanding. A screwup. And I've hated myself for it ever since."

Heather couldn't meet her gaze. She stared down at the floor, totally unprepared to have this conversation, totally caught off guard. Still, despite the swirl of conflicting emotion, she knew what she wanted to say. Yes. . . after everything she'd been through with Ed—after almost having gotten Ed killed with that stupid skating dare, she knew exactly what she wanted to say.

"Well, I can't forgive you," she breathed. "But I know what it's like to do something totally unforgivable, and to wish to more than anything in the world you could take back." The words stuck in her throat. "I know what that's like."

Gaia nodded. "It sucks," she said simply.

Heather laughed and glanced up. "Yeah." She sniffed. "You know—"

The door burst open. *Jesus.* Ed leaned into the

bathroom on his crutches. His eyes darted between the two of them. "Man," he said. "This is so weird."

Heather rolled her eyes.

"We know," Gaia groaned. "Can we move on, please?"

"Right," Ed said. He turned to Gaia. "I *really* need to talk to you before you go. I mean, now. I need to talk to you now."

Gaia frowned at him, then nodded. She followed him out of the bathroom. Ed turned back to Heather.

"You doing okay?" he asked.

Heather braved a smile. There was concern in his question, genuine concern—but no hint of the old connection between them. Maybe she'd wanted to see it so badly that she'd been projecting it on him all day. But she believed that they could start by building a real friendship, a new foundation—*Give it up.* It was pathetic. She was just deluding herself. She wanted Ed. And she would never have him. She'd blown it. Case closed.

"I'm fine," she lied. "You go ahead."

"Cool," Ed said. He barely looked at her as he slammed the bathroom door.

Heather turned back to the mirror. She blinked twice. Tears began to fall into the sink. She turned on the water and scrubbed her face harshly with soap. If Heather wanted to help Ed and complete her transformation into Gaia Moore, then she would have to wash her mask away. The problem was that she didn't know what lay beneath it anymore.

The Demon

THE SECOND ED SLAMMED HIS PARents' bedroom door shut, he began to have second thoughts. He had known this would happen. He shook his head and paced back and forth on his crutches while Gaia eased herself down on the foot of the bed, staring at him the way people stare at dangerous lunatics on the subway. He couldn't let this nervous energy go, though. He had to keep feeding off the adrenaline—no matter how sick it made him, no matter how manic he appeared. He couldn't put this off anymore. Now was the time. Before Gaia went out into the street, quite possibly never to return.

"What is going on?" Gaia asked impatiently. "We all need to get ready, Ed."

"I know," Ed muttered. He kept pacing. The crutches dug into his armpits, chafing his skin. He hardly noticed. "That's why I need to talk to you."

"So talk," Gaia replied.

Nice. Well, he could always count on her to be blunt, that was for damn sure. "The thing is this," he began. Then he stopped. His face burned with the embarrassment of a five-year-old. Never in his life had he felt like such a toddler. Not even when he *was* a toddler. The sooner he did it, the sooner it would be done.

"The thing is *what?*" Gaia pressed.

"This is the thing, I'm so worried about you going out there, Gaia." He was still procrastinating, but he couldn't help himself. Aside from skating and cracking inappropriate jokes, procrastinating was one of his greatest talents. It was one of the few things he could always fall back on. "We both know the stakes here. I mean, it's so dangerous, I'm having a lot of trouble letting you—"

"We've been over this, Ed," she interrupted, but her tone was softer. "You have to let me go, okay?"

"I know, I know," he muttered. Finally he stopped pacing and turned to her. "Look, I know you're going out there to save Sam, and I know you *will.* And I know what he means to you, and I know this is the wrong to time to say this, but I have to say it, Gaia. I have to. Because what if I don't have another chance to say it? I don't know if I'll see you again, but if I don't, I could never live with myself—"

"Ed, you're babbling," Gaia interrupted. She smiled and arched an eyebrow.

"I love you," Ed blurted.

Her smile vanished. Ed's pulse was racing. The sound of it filled his ears. She wasn't reacting. Her expression was utterly blank. Maybe he'd made a big mistake. But no; he'd done the right thing—no matter how painful the consequences. Even if she stood and bolted from the room (which seemed a very likely possibility), he'd freed himself. He'd exorcised the demon. The secret that had been festering inside him was finally out, whether it meant anything to her or not.

"I am in love with you," he continued, suddenly consumed with a strange, brazen confidence. Maybe it was just that his inner torment had ended at last. "Not puppy love, not platonic love, not any of that shit. I have been in love with you since the first day I saw you—since the first day you saw me in the chair, and you still treated me like you'd treat any other asshole. And I love you even more now than I did then. And if I see you again after today, I'll love you more then than I do now."

Gaia started shaking her head. Her face went visibly pale. Her lips parted, standing out in stark red relief against her white skin. "I should. . ." The words were hoarse, barely comprehensible. "I should have. . ."

"What?" Ed pressed. The confidence subsided as quickly as it had appeared—and now anxiety threatened to strangle him. "What?"

She stared into his eyes. "I should have run away yesterday. But I couldn't. Because of you. I don't know what I'd do without you. I mean, I don't know what I'd *be* without you." Now *she* was babbling. But her incoherent jumble of words was the sweetest music Ed had ever heard. "I think that I…"

Ed suddenly realized that he had pitched forward on his crutches so much that he was in danger of falling over. He straightened, every single cell in his body poised to hear her finish that sentence—the sentence that could quite possibly make the impossible a reality, that would even make the danger that awaited them seem insignificant. . . .

But then, something shifted behind her eyes.

"I think that I should get going," she finished.

A long breath flowed from Ed's lungs. So. He'd been dreaming. Not that he was surprised. It was okay, though. Yes. As long as she could stay alive, Ed could live with everything else. The rest would work itself out later. He nodded and flashed her a quick smile, then turned and opened the bedroom door.

"I don't believe it," he breathed.

Had he not been in grave danger, had Gaia not just broken his heart for the hundredth time. . . well, the sight that greeted his eyes would have seemed like some incredible, erotic fantasy come to life. Because standing there, in a small semi-circle in front of the door, were five Gaias. Five carbon copies of the same girl. Clones. The realization sent a terrible chill down his spine. Loki wanted clones, and now he was getting them. It was beyond perverse. There wasn't a word for it.

Gaia appeared at his side. "You're sure you all want to do this?" she asked the FOHs as they slipped into army jackets and black sunglasses.

"Beats going to class," Megan said.

The others giggled. Even Heather.

Ed swallowed. He'd explained the danger to all of them—as had Gaia—but he had a feeling they hadn't thought much past putting on the outfits. They saw it as more of a game. Which, in the long run, was probably a good thing.

"*God,* we kick ass," Carrie murmured.

Megan grinned at her. "I am *totally* keeping these pants—"

"Okay, okay," Gaia interrupted gently. "Let's do it." She hesitated, then took a moment to look each of them in the face. "I can't thank you enough. You have no idea how much you're helping me. I—I was wrong about you. All of you."

"What*ever,*" Megan said with a laugh. "This is exciting! It's like, so glamorous or something. Like playing spies. I don't know. It's cool."

Gaia nodded. Her smile grew pained.

Ed's body went numb. They really *didn't* have any idea what they were about to do, did they? But that was okay. `Their ignorance would protect them.` Or so Ed desperately prayed. No, at this point, they could only hope that Loki wouldn't hurt somebody who knew nothing. Why would he? It wouldn't do him any good. He watched as Heather handed Gaia the last army jacket and pair of black sunglasses. Then

Gaia strode forward and opened Ed's door.

"Gaia," Ed began. "I—"

"I'll be back," she promised again.

And then she was gone.

Telltale Clues

TOM WAS CERTAIN THAT HE WAS dreaming. He must have fallen asleep while on watch in his car. He jerked upright, biting down hard on the inside of his cheek.

The pain was real.

He could taste salty blood in his mouth. It sent a surge of joy through him.

Gaia was *there*: alive and well, not twenty feet away from his parked car. She was standing tall, her long blond hair cascading over her shoulders—dressed in those old clothes she loved so much: the tank top, the ratty army pants, the jacket. . . . She was real. All he needed to do was hustle her safely to his car.

He threw open the door, then froze. His joy turned to instant horror.

Walking out of Ed Fargo's lobby was Gaia. *Another Gaia.* Dressed the same way. Then came another. And then another. And then another. . . until there were six

Gaias standing on the sidewalk in a loose huddle. All identical. All dressed in the exact same outfits, with the exact same sunglasses. Tom's eyes narrowed, searching for subtle differences. To his relief, there *were* a few: the girls were of differing heights and body types. Some were taller than others. Some were more slender. So there was no way. . . there was no way his twin could have cloned her already. Cloning meant producing a *newborn,* not a fully developed human being.

Didn't it?

The answer made no difference. He thrust the thoughts aside; they were born of panic and irrationality. Tom had covered every possible base since he'd spoken with Ed. Loki could not have gotten to her yet. This was something else. It had to be something else. Something Gaia had concocted.

And then it hit him.

Decoys.

Of course. His daughter was absolutely brilliant. She was attempting to escape—

Without any warning, the six Gaias dispersed. They sprinted toward the intersection and fanned off in six different directions. Instant chaos ensued. The other two black sedans peeled off the curb, nearly crashing into each other with a loud screech. His colleagues were clearly just as baffled as he was.

Focus, Tom, focus!

He slammed the door shut, then turned the ignition—his eyes zeroing in on each of the girls for less than a tenth of a second at a time, searching for the telltale clues that couldn't be mimicked: the graceful gait, the musculature. . . and most of all, the training. The real Gaia would keep her eyes in front of her. The real Gaia would use her surroundings to get a complete picture of any potential threats—a car mirror, a storefront window, whatever was at hand.

There.

Yes, the one who was already furthest from the lobby, halfway down the next block. The one staring at her feet. He slammed his foot down on the gas pedal, not taking his eyes off her even for an instant. But she was too damn fast. It was nearly impossible to maneuver the car and keep watching her. The last thing he needed was to hit some innocent pedestrian, and ruin all three of their lives. . . .

She turned the corner at Second Avenue. Downtown.

Damn it. Tom was forced to run a red light. He swerved, nearly colliding with a double-decker tourist bus. A horn blared. He didn't hear it. He kept close to the curb. There was only Gaia. She ducked into an alley on East Second Street.

He almost smiled. He should have known she would go for an alley; now there was no way to follow her by car. He slammed on the brakes. The deafening screech shattered the early-afternoon calm. At least five people ran for cover on the street, turning to look at him. It was a risk to attract such attention to himself, but an acceptable one. He jumped from his car and ran after her. Nobody would get a good look at his face; they were all too stunned. And should the idling car be towed, it was untraceable.

"Gaia!" he shouted.

The green jacket flew behind her like a cape. She was so close, maybe thirty feet away. And running toward a dead end: a brick wall, laced with obscene graffiti.

"Gaia, please!" he gasped. He dug down for any more strength he could muster from his legs, pulling within just a few feet of her. "It's me. Your father. . ."

She ignored him completely. But she was forced to slow down. The wall blocked her path. Her head darted left, then right. With no other choices left, Tom took two hard steps and jumped headfirst for his daughter, tackling her to the rugged pavement.

"Ow!" she shrieked.

That voice.

Tom rolled off her, scrambling to his feet. To his utter horror, he found himself staring into a pair of hazel eyes, capped by a crooked wig. It was the face of a stranger.

"No," he hissed out loud. "No. . ."

"What's the matter?" the girl snarled. "Not who you expected to see?" She smiled, then stood and dusted herself off. “That hurt. You should really be more careful.” She peered over his shoulder, back toward the street. “Maybe I should call the cops or something. I mean, you, like, *attacked* me.”

Dread threatened to smother him, to bring him to his knees. He’d lost her. And he knew the reason. He’d spent so much time away from her that he *couldn’t* spot the telltale clues anymore. He’d failed her yet again.

His cell phone started ringing. George, no doubt.

“See ya,” the girl muttered, hurrying away from him.

Tom grabbed the phone from his suit pocket, watching the girl go. “George,” he gasped, still trying to catch his breath. “I’ve lost her—”

“She’s headed for the Chelsea loft right now,” George interrupted. “We have confirmation. Meet me there.”

Tom opened his mouth, but George hung up—before Tom had a chance to tell him that in this case, confirmation meant absolutely nothing.

Today, for the very first time, I saw the truth. Many truths, actually.

I'm not in Ed's heart anymore. Not a trace of me. He's in love with Gaia. More than he ever was with me. It's in everything he says, any exchange at all; two words, one word—it doesn't matter. It's in his eyes. And she loves him just as much. She hides it better, but it's still so obvious. I hope she's not trying to hide it from Ed because that would be the most screwed-up waste of a relationship.

I can't even believe I'd let myself say something that cheesy about *anybody*, much less about the two of them. But the thing I realized in Ed's bathroom, after they left me there alone, was that. . . I *can.* I don't know what it is, but I think that maybe the truth finally cut through because I was finally ready to accept it. After the first few seconds of being alone in there, a new feeling

started to take over. It started to feel like I was kind of washing the old Heather away. Officially. I scraped all the self-pitying skin from my face, and I had this kind of revelation.

Maybe helping Gaia wasn't the most selfless thing I could do. After all, I used it as an opportunity to dazzle my own friends. To regain my social status. I'd been hiding too much for too long—my family's money problems, my trouble with Ed, my sister's anorexia. . . . The truth is, I was sick of drifting apart from the people I need most. I needed to assert myself again. Hey guys, want to do something really far out and crazy? And skip school at the same time? And pretend to be Gaia Moore, beautiful and mysterious freak of nature? And they went for it. It was just the right thing at just the right time. I was helping myself, and I know it.

So maybe the *most* selfless thing I could do—the only way I could truly make up for all the self-serving ways I'd manipulated Ed—was to give up Ed himself.

And I guess, without really saying anything in the last moment in the bathroom. . . I guess that's what I did. I let him go.

Which really, really sucks.

Gaia could
only stand
and watch,
immobilized.
Never
before
had she
felt like
such a
failure.

IN SPITE OF THE OVERWHELMING odds against her, Gaia knew she had one advantage: she was alone. She could hide more easily and attack with greater surprise. True, she'd been invited. True, Loki was expecting her. But the other "Gaias" had hopefully confused him. Just a little. Just long enough for her to pounce.

Confusion

As she crept toward the rear of the nondescript warehouse-turned-loft from an alley on 26th Street, her gaze swept in either direction. The front of the building may have been ornate and majestic, but the back façade was a decrepit display of neglect—especially at the ground level, where the windows were black with soot, or cracked. Loki's men were nowhere to be seen. She crouched beside a basement window, smashed it with her foot, then climbed carefully through the jagged remains and dropped down into a deserted boiler room. Moving swiftly and silently, she ran through a maze of dank, narrow hallways until she found an entrance to a side staircase.

Hold on, Sam, she silently pleaded, dashing up stairwell after stairwell. *I'm almost there. . . .*

When she reached the fifth-floor landing, she stopped dead in her tracks.

So much for being alone. She could not believe what she saw—or rather, *who* she saw standing at the door. It was her uncle, dressed as always in an impeccable dark suit. The hard, deep-set blue eyes were unmistakable. Her father's eyes were softer. Not that they concealed any less. It was just the luck of the genetic draw, a twist of fate.

"*Gaia?*" Oliver whispered, sounding just as surprised as she felt. His voice was tremulous. "What are you doing here?"

He stood with his back against the hallway door and a pistol in his hand—flanked on either side by two faceless, heavyset men in leather jackets and black pants. They were also armed. Gaia didn't get it. What the hell was going on? Didn't he know she was coming? Unless. . . *he isn't Loki.* But he still would have known about the loft, wouldn't he? Confusion overwhelmed her. She couldn't even muster a reply.

"You've got to get out of here," Oliver whispered urgently. "It's not safe."

"I. . ." Gaia stammered, not even knowing where to begin.

Oliver brought his finger to his lips, imploring her to stay quiet. "Please, Gaia," he whispered, "You need to go. You can't be here now. Loki is in one of the lofts down the hall, and we think he may be holding Sam Moon hostage in there. Please, just wait downstairs for me and let my people handle Loki."

Gaia shook her head. She may not have understood what was going on, but she was certain of one thing. "If Sam is in there, then I'm going in too," she said.

The two men exchanged angry looks.

"Gaia, *please,*" Oliver begged. "Don't do this. It's too dangerous."

"Forget it," she replied.

Oliver stared back at her. His finger nervously danced over the trigger of his gun. The men shook their heads, as if telling him, *Get rid of her.* Then he sighed.

"Look, I don't have time to argue," he breathed. "Just stay behind us, do you understand? I'm not going to let him hurt you."

Gaia nodded.

Oliver took a deep breath and then turned to his people. "All right," he whispered, opening the hallway door slowly. "When I give the signal, we go in."

Warning

TOM'S MIND WAS CLEAR AS A NEWLY sharpened blade. He was barely aware of screeching up behind George and leaping from his car in front of Loki's newest residence. George shouted something at him—some kind of warning, no doubt—but Tom tuned him out. His thoughts had been reduced to a single image: that of his twin's face. The face of a man who would soon be dead.

Adrenaline kicked in as Tom flung open the door to the main stairwell and bounded up the creaky wooden stairs, taking them in threes and fours. In less than fifteen seconds, he'd reached the fifth floor. His eyes homed in on apartment #53. He didn't slow down. Instead, he took all his momentum from his mad sprint and channeled it into a vicious side kick into the door.

"Hai!"

But the door gave absolutely no resistance.

It slammed against the inner wall of the apartment with a thunderous crack, and then creaked slowly back towards him.

There had been no need to break it down. It was already open.

Tom hesitated.

"Gaia?" he called. Gaia?"

There was no response. He fought to catch his breath as he took a cursory look around Loki's living room. But there was nothing to find. The place was empty. All the windows were open. A light breeze rustled his hair. There were hardly any furnishings, even—just two chairs and a glass coffee table. And that made Tom extremely uneasy. Something was unquestionably wrong.

He closed the door behind him and hurried toward a side entrance. Footsteps floated to him from the hallway just on the other side of the door. . . then ceased.

That's got to be him.

Ducking down, Tom reached into his vest holster and pulled out his gun, aiming it defensively at the side door. If Loki—

The door crashed open. Tom cocked his pistol, searching for a target—but his joints suddenly seized in panic. *Gaia?* She was right behind Loki and two other men. . . no, this was impossible. He stood, and found three pistols in his face. Loki's muzzle was the closest, barely inches from his nose. Before Tom could even exhale, the front door flew open behind him, striking the wall again. A young man with black hair and chiseled features stepped inside, wielding a machine gun—which he promptly aimed. . . at Loki?

This is crazy.

Tom's eyes flashed in bewilderment between the machine gun and his brother. This young man didn't work for the agency. Maybe there was some kind of betrayal afoot, but he never—

"Drop the gun, Loki!" Oliver shouted.

Tom blinked. Bewilderment turned to horror. "*What?*"

"You heard me, Loki!" Oliver spat. "I said drop it."

Gaia stepped forward, thrusting herself between Oliver and one of the men. "Where is Sam?" she demanded. "Tell me where he is, or I swear to God, I'll kill you."

Blood pounded in Tom's temples. He couldn't make sense of any of this. He'd fallen into some nightmarish alternate universe where no certainties applied—apparently, not even those of life and death. "Gaia, what—what are you talking about?" he gasped.

Oliver turned his gun toward the young man standing behind Tom—the man Tom didn't even know. "You," he said, staring intensely. "Drop it."

The young man obeyed, dropping his machine gun to the floor and raising his hands. Oliver turned back to Tom. "Now you, Loki. Drop it."

Just as Tom began lowering his gun, Gaia burst forward and grabbed him by his jacket lapels, shaking him violently. "Tell me where he is!" she screamed again. "Tell me where Sam is now!"

"Gaia, don't!" Oliver warned her. "Step away from him. He's too dangerous. Drop that gun, Loki. I'm not going to warn you again."

Tom gaped at his daughter's distraught face. He was beginning to make sense of the situation. Loki had set a trap. And Tom had fallen right it—as had Gaia. Rage boiled in the center of Tom's chest, but the pain in Gaia's eyes commanded all his attention. All that hysteria and anger. . . all of it directed at him. Tom dropped his gun to the floor and grabbed Gaia's shoulders, fighting to keep her still.

"Gaia," he said sharply. "Gaia, it's *me.* I don't know what kind of sick setup he's created here, but that's what this is, *a setup*. I'm not Loki, I'm your father."

"Shut your mouth," she howled, shoving him in the chest. "No more lies! Just tell me where Sam is. Tell me where he is."

It struck him then, with the force of a bullet: She didn't know. She didn't know that Sam was dead. In all the chaos, Tom hadn't really heard the question she'd kept asking of him. But now he was beginning to understand just how far Loki had gone to deceive her. He truly had no limits. Nothing was too cruel. So Tom had to tell her the truth. In spite of the madness swirling through the room, in spite of the fact that he probably only had seconds to live, he had to tell her.

"Gaia, Sam is dead," he whispered. "I'm so sorry—"

"You sick son of a bitch," Oliver barked. "You already killed him, didn't you?"

Gaia went still. Very suddenly. Every ounce of life seemed to drop from her face. Tom found himself wishing, like a naïve child, that his brother had never existed—that there had never been an Oliver to torture people so unmercifully, to inflict so much pain. He was a true sociopath. People's feelings were all part of the game to him, even the feelings of those he claimed to love. He wasn't even human. So there was no way for any human to compete. Except to keep telling the truth.

"Gaia, listen to me," Tom said firmly. "Oliver is

lying. *He* is Loki, and he, or one of his people, shot Sam last night in the alley behind the Bubble Lounge."

Oliver stepped forward and thrust the silencer against Tom's cheek. The metal was cold and hard; it scraped against his bone. "This man is a liar," Oliver hissed through clenched teeth.

Tom had to ignore him. He had to ignore the gun. The need for truth took precedent over the need for resistance, or even the need for life. He looked deep into Gaia's shattered blue eyes, holding her gaze as best he could. "I wish you could have found out any other way. I'm telling you the truth, Gaia—"

"Step away from him, sweetheart," Oliver commanded.

Gaia obeyed.

One simple motion. That was all. But it was a move that terrified Tom far more than the gun buried in his flesh. Because he knew then that he had lost. He had lost his daughter forever.

Endless Lies

GAIA REALIZED SOMETHING IN THAT instant: she'd been wrong about her father's eyes. They were not softer than her uncle's. They were just as hard. In fact, she couldn't even tell the two men apart. They were both dressed in the exact same suit. Their hair, their faces, even their *voices*. . . all of it, exactly the same. As were their endless lies and accusations. Every word they uttered was aimed at winning her trust, and every word yielded the opposite result. Loving gestures were sadistic, and vice versa.

So. The conclusion she drew was obvious. She couldn't trust either one of them to tell her the truth about Sam. Not for a moment. If she were going to get the truth about him, then she would have to get it from someone else. And there was only one other person in the room: conveniently, the one person she'd been waiting to see since this morning. Her eyes flashed across the room to Josh.

And then she frowned.

His face was as immaculate as ever. Totally unblemished. Not the slightest bruise or the slightest bit of swelling. Not even a scratch. It was impossible. She'd smashed it to a bloody pulp only hours ago.

Only then did she notice he was staring back at her.

That heinous smirk spread across his lips—the same one he'd worn even as she'd pummeled him and demanded to know Sam's fate. Gaia's muscles tensed. That reminded her: she'd made a promise to herself. She'd vowed to finish what she had started earlier today. Josh knew if Sam was dead or alive. She could see it in every repugnant feature. He'd always known. He'd known the answer every time she'd asked the question, even when she'd tried to beat it out of him. And now he was going to tell her. Because she simply didn't care anymore. For Josh, she was throwing out all the rules of conduct—every honorable aspect of battle she'd learned from the Go Rin No Sho. He deserved no less. He was going to answer her, and then he was going to die.

"*You* tell me," Gaia spat. She strode across the room and planted herself in front of Josh so that they were practically nose-to-nose. "I know you know the truth, Josh. Is Sam dead or not?"

Her father or her uncle said something behind her, but she didn't hear it. They ceased to exist. Nothing existed except Gaia and Josh.

"You're not going to tell me?" she asked calmly.

Josh's smile widened.

Gaia's hand darted to his face—so quickly that it made a *whir* as it sliced through the air. Josh didn't have a prayer of reacting. He was still smiling, in fact, when she clamped her fingers around the back of his skull and slammed it into Loki's glass breakfast table. The room exploded with the sound of shattering glass. Gaia didn't even flinch. Blood splattered everywhere: the floor, the walls, Gaia's tank top, her fatigues. Nobody moved. Nobody made a sound.

The smile was finally gone.

Gaia crouched beside Josh and grabbed a tuft of that spiky black hair, lifting his destroyed face with a harsh tug. Shards of coffee table dangled from his cheek.

"Dead or alive, Josh?" she whispered.

He didn't answer. Instead, he jerked his head away and lunged at her, butting her in the gut and sending her sprawling to the floor.

"Gaia!" her father and uncle shrieked at the same time.

Josh jumped to his feet, aiming a sweeping kick at her head. But she ducked the kick easily, coming back at him with a hard punch to the stomach followed by a vicious combination of blows to the chest—ending with a roundhouse kick that slammed his entire body up against the wall. She pinned him there, breathing heavily. She could hear them yelling to stop, but nobody stepped in. Either they didn't care enough about Josh, or they were just terrified of getting anywhere near *her*. Which was just what she wanted.

"Tell me the truth, Josh," she hissed.

He spat his blood into her face. "You *bitch,*" he croaked through his swollen lips. He clumsily swung at her head—clearly dazed and disoriented. Gaia didn't even bother to block the punch. She was sending him a message: *You aren't even worth the effort.* Instead she whirled and grabbed him by the neck, hauling him toward one of the huge, open windows. There was no stopping her now. She finally had a clear target for all her pent-up rage. She didn't know what she wanted more: the truth about Sam or the end of Josh's life. He struggled feebly. Gaia kneed him in the solar plexus. His body sagged. She was forced to drag him like a sack of potatoes.

"You should have told me, Josh," she grunted, hoisting his body up onto the windowsill. "Unless you want to tell me now? Last chance to tell me." She held him by his shirt—allowing him to lean perilously into open space.

"Gaia, please," someone pleaded. "Stop this—"

"Okay," Josh moaned. "Okay." He raised his hands in submission. "Okay."

The words suddenly snapped her out of her frenzy. She realized that she *did* want the truth more than she wanted to kill him. She yanked him back inside, standing his teetering body on his feet and holding him there.

"Okay, what?" she demanded.

Josh turned towards her father and her uncle. For the first time ever, she saw fear in his eyes. "Jesus, will you just tell her?" he pleaded. His voice was muffled and distorted by the damage to his mouth. "Just tell her the truth!"

Gaia turned around to follow his line of sight.

He was talking to Oliver. *Not* her father.

"We've already accomplished everything," Josh mumbled. "*She's* here. We've got her. *He's* here. We've *won*. Just tell her—"

Thwip.

Oliver interrupted him with a bullet. Josh's body instantly went limp in Gaia's arms. Her jaw dropped. There was a smoking black hole in the center of his head. It was in the exact same spot as the laser target on Sam's head had been.

It had taken less than a second, but that one shot told Gaia everything she'd needed to know. Oliver was Loki. Oliver was the liar. And Sam was dead.

Happiness

TOM HAD NO TIME TO THINK. HE'D just watched his brother kill a man in cold blood only inches from Gaia, and he was quite sure Gaia was next. Aggression took over. He dove for Loki, but his twin was too quick. The silencer was at his cheek before he could close the gap between them.

"Don't be ridiculous, Tom" Loki murmured. "Do you really think I would ever hurt Gaia? She's practically my daughter. She should have *been* my daughter. I would never harm a hair on her head. She knows that. She knows how much I love her. Don't you, sweetheart?"

He turned to Gaia, shoving the gun into Tom's

flesh. Gaia stared coldly at him, nodding her head in the affirmative. Her face was unreadable. She knew how careful she needed to be. Even in these last moments, her caution made Tom proud.

"So, Tom," Loki went on. He affected that deliberately bored tone he always used when he tried to mask anger. "I'm sure there must be hordes of federal agents waiting right outside that door, ready to swoop in here and bring justice to the world. But they don't really know the first thing about justice, do they? They don't know what you've done to me. They have no idea that true justice can only be served until I am living the life that is rightfully mine."

I have to keep him talking, Tom realized. It was the only way to buy time. Fortunately, Loki loved to hear himself speak. Particularly when he felt he could gloat over a victory. Tom's gaze remained fixed straight ahead, but Gaia began to inch out of his line of sight. He forced himself to breathe evenly. He couldn't follow her with his eyes, no matter how desperately he wanted to.

"Why do you think I'm wearing the same clothes as you, Tom?" Loki asked. "You're nearly as bright as me. I'm sure you're beginning to understand. The agents will swoop in heroically to take down Loki. But this time, they won't have to take Loki to jail, because Loki will be *dead.* Tom will be forced to kill him. You see? It's quite beautiful, really. The case will be closed, and Tom and his daughter will walk out of here and live happily ever after."

Tom's eyes flashed to his brother—and for the first time, he realized that they were dressed in identical suits. His insides turned to liquid. Never in his life had he felt like such a fool. His brother had planned this entire scenario from the moment Tom had returned to New York. Plans within plans within plans. . . every one of them designed to make Tom more desperate, to lure him to this place, to let his anger cloud his reason—exactly where Loki wanted him.

"I'll tell you the truth, Tom," Loki added. His tone softened. "I'm tired of living underground. So tired. And I'm sure you are too."

Tom nodded, just barely. Sweat broke out on his forehead, trickling down to the gun. "Truer words were never spoken," he whispered.

"Well this is going to help us *both*," Loki stated, without a trace of irony. "We'll put you out of your misery, and I can live the life you've wanted *for* you, you see? Money only buys so much happiness, after all."

In another life, in another world, Tom might have felt sad for his brother. But now there was no sadness; there was no pity. Only hate.

"Good-bye, brother," Loki murmured.

Tom squeezed his eyes shut, steeling himself for death.

Instead, the barrel flew from his cheek. *Thwip! Thwip!* Shots rang out, but not at Tom. His eyes opened. Gaia had jumped between them, kicking the gun from Loki's hand. Tom did not waste another second. He leaped straight at his brother, ramming his shoulder into his midsection and wrestling him to the ground—just as he caught a glimpse of a mass of black boots storming into the apartment. Just as Loki had assumed, George and a full team of agents had been waiting for a signal, a sign—anything to indicate that the raid should begin. And Loki himself had provided it with the gunshots.

Agonizing pain tore through Tom's midsection as Loki crammed his knee into the soft part of his stomach, then flipped him over, grasping Tom's neck. He couldn't breathe. Blood surged to his head. *Not good.* With his last bit of strength, Tom swatted his brother's hands away and kicked Loki out from under him, reversing their positions, pinning his arms to the ground. Triumph welled inside him. Now he would—

"George!" Loki called. "Can't move, he's got my arms pinned down. He's got two men, do you have them?"

"We've got them, Tom," George replied.

Tom's eyes widened. He shook his head violently. "No, George! I'm Tom."

There was no response.

My God. They have no idea who is who. His concentration wavered—and it was just enough for Loki to flip him again. Tom struggled, but he couldn't move.

"It's okay," Loki called out breathlessly. He gazed into his brother's eyes, smiling, "I've got him. I've got him now."

Failure

GAIA STARED AT THE TWO MEN ON the floor. Everything had happened so fast. Too fast. She'd kicked the gun away—but by the time she'd regained her balance, they were already rolling in each other's arms. Her thoughts melted into cool, black nothingness. Energy hummed in her veins. She knew she should have been absolutely terrified. She couldn't tell them apart.

"It's your call, George," one of the agents shouted urgently. "What's the deal?"

"I. . . I. . ."

Gaia turned to him. George's face had never looked more weathered and defeated than at this moment.

"Gaia? We need your help here. . . ."

"I don't—I don't know," Gaia stammered.

"We'll have to take them both," another agent shouted. They formed a tight circle around the struggle, weapons aimed at the both of them.

"I'm Tom," one of them insisted.

"He's lying!" the other immediately countered.

"That's it," the agent announced. "Take 'em both."

The agents jumped into the struggle and ripped the two men away from each other—but one of them broke free long enough to break for the door. He bounced off two of the armed men, dodged the grip of another, and slipped through the door.

"Don't shoot!" George cried.

Gaia could only stand and watch, immobilized. Never before had she felt like such a failure. And her exploits with Josh were beginning to take their toll. Her limbs grew heavy. Her vision dimmed.

Three agents raced chased after him.

"Dad?" Gaia called, staggering through the mob of agents.

"Don't worry, Gaia." His voice echoed up through the stairwell. "It will be okay. I'll come for you, I swear. I love you—"

"I'm here, Gaia," the other one interrupted. Gaia whirled. He was being shackled in handcuffs. "I'm right here, sweetheart. Just stay with me, Gaia. Stay close. I'm not letting you out of my sight again. Ever."

Gaia looked at him. She had absolutely no idea what to think. She was *so* sick of this—so sick of trying to figure out who was who. It was easier when she didn't care. Easier when she'd despised them both.

"Gaia?" he said sweetly.

It was too much. It was all too much. There was no way she would be dragged to some godforsaken cell to answer questions from a bunch of clueless federal agents. Yes, Gaia saw her future from this moment. And it made her physically ill.

So she ran.

"Gaia, *no!*" she heard him pleading as she bolted for the stairs. "No! Stay with me, Gaia. Please. . . stay. . ."

Thankfully, his voice was drowned out by the clattering of her footsteps.

Sam is dead.

Sam, to whom I bared as much of my soul as I could. Sam, with whom there were so many perfect fantasies. Sam, with whom nothing ever truly worked.

I'd spent all that time dying to know that he was safe. And he was already gone. He died for me. And I can't thank him. There's no point in trying to describe what I feel, because that would only dishonor his memory. Words, words, words, right? Sam Moon deserves more than words. He deserves his life back.

And I can't give that to him.

I had fallen out of love with him in so many ways. But now I can't even remember why. All that's left is the part of me that still loves him. The part of me that always will love him. I wish I'd known him better. I know that must sound strange to have loved someone so much and not really have known him, but I know now that it is possible. I

fell in love with him without knowing him, and the catastrophe that is my life forced me to keep it that way. To *really* know him would have been an amazing privilege. Because Sam Moon was remarkable. And when all is said and done, there really are not that many remarkable people. There are even fewer heroes. Sam was a hero, as well.

But I'm using words, aren't I?

I wish we'd just skipped each other at the chess tables that rainy day. I wish he was still just the beautiful mystery man I never knew. The one I hated, precisely because I found him so attractive.

So it's time for me to leave. It's like Heather said: it's time to flush my past down the toilet. Because I'm sick of myself, too. I have to start from scratch somewhere else. I have no idea whether my father or Loki made it out of that loft, but I can't think about that right now. I have to leave all my enemies and all my guardians behind.

It's time to start the normal life I've been secretly dreaming about.

Of all the lives I could lead, I know I'd be happiest as a waitress. A waitress in some truck stop diner in Anywhere, USA, where everyone knows your name but no one asks you any big personal questions. It's time to go do that now. I'm sure of it.

There's only one other thing I know for sure. I want Ed to leave with me. Whatever that means. I don't know what it means. Right now it can't mean anything. Right now I need to grieve, and I know Ed will understand that. But Ed is the only friend I have left in this world. The only person I can absolutely trust. The only person who actually understands me. And somewhere, far down the line, that might mean everything.

So that's where all my roaming is going to lead me. To Ed's

house. I’m going to go to Ed’s house, and I’m going to ask him to leave with me.

And I hope to God he says yes.

But I know he won’t.

The only
thing Gaia
was sure
of was that
she was not
afraid. She
just didn’t
know if that
was a good
thing or a
bad thing.

IT WAS NEARLY TWO A.M. BY THE time Gaia rounded the corner to Ed's building.

No Fear

She'd rehearsed what she would say a hundred times as she'd roamed the streets, but nothing sounded right. It was a simple enough request: *Ed, run away with me.* But somehow, that didn't sound right. Somehow, it didn't convey what she truly felt. The real problem was, she couldn't put her finger on the feeling. Only that it consumed her.

So she was going to have to wing it.

At least she'd kept her promise. She'd sworn she would come back, and here she was. They could go from there. . . .

Gaia stopped walking.

She stopped thinking altogether. Her heart seemed to sink, then break, then seemed to disappear completely. She should have known what she would find just outside Ed's lobby. Not Ed's parents, or his sister, or Heather, or the FOHs—or Ed himself, out for a late-night walk. No, instead she found only what she had come to expect from life: something sad and dark and miserable. . . a reminder of the futility of hoping for the future.

There were three men in black ahead of her.

What had made her think she could get away? Why

had she bothered to incorporate even the *concept* of hope into her life? It was always a mirage. Always. Loki was never going to let go, and Gaia was never going to have peace. These were the two commandments of Gaia's existence.

It was only a moment before they spotted her and began to walk toward her. She didn't bother to run. There was no point anymore. `The running was over.` But as they drew closer, she could not help but stare at their leader. Because he looked so very much like. . .

Josh.

She blinked. It wasn't possible. He'd collapsed right in her arms. Dead. With a smoking bullet lodged in the center of his head. No. But whether he existed or not, he was closing in on her while she was wasting time deliberating. Whoever he was, Gaia needed to get away from him, and she needed to do it now. She finally turned herself around. But three more thugs approached her from the opposite direction, cutting her off.

Of course. Loki wasn't about to make the same mistake twice. He wasn't about to lose her again. He had her cornered and outnumbered. Not to mention haunted. Gaia came to a stop in the middle of the street, and tried to assess her options. She could fight them all off, but there were surely more of them around the next corner, and the next. *Think!* Loki had her in goddamn checkmate. He was about to win his own stupid endless cruel game, and there was nothing Gaia could do about it—

A black Mercedes suddenly careened around the corner, screeching to a halt in the middle of the street. It swerved up onto the curb beside her. The passenger door swung open. She peered inside. It was *him.* Whoever he was.

"Get in."

Gaia hesitated. Josh and the mob were closing in.

"Gaia, it's me," he said urgently. "You know it's me."

She took a step closer, but it was so dark.

"There's no time," he said. "You have to trust me, Gaia, please. Look in my eyes. You know I'm your father."

Gaia leaned forward and peered into the shadowy car. A pair of blue eyes stared back at her. They were soft, very soft. . . and glittering. They seemed to promise peace. It was a lie, to be sure, but she didn't care anymore. Her body took charge. She leaped from the sidewalk into the car at the very moment Josh lunged for her legs, falling to the street. Her father slammed on the gas pedal. Fists pounded on the dark windows and roof as they sped away.

"Are you okay?" he gasped.

But Gaia didn't answer. She swung her head around and watched helplessly as Ed's building grew smaller and smaller, and then disappeared into the distance.

"Good-bye," she murmured. She had to be numb right now. Because if she let herself feel everything she'd just lost, she wouldn't be able to live. She turned back to her father. Staring at his profile as the buildings zoomed by in the background, she truly wasn't sure if he was her father or not.

The only thing Gaia was sure of was that she was not afraid. She just didn't know if that was a good thing or a bad thing.

here is a sneak peek of Fearless™ #19: TWINS

I've never told anyone this before, but for the first five years of my life—before the specialists could figure out what the hell was wrong with me—my parents considered the possibility that I might be mentally challenged. You know, "slow."

See, I kept doing all these things that seemed extraordinarily stupid, and my parents could not figure out why. My mother had been top of her class at the University of Moscow. My father tested at the genius level. It wouldn't make sense for their only child to be a moron.

Of course, certain signs pointed to the fact that I was smarter than I acted. I picked up languages really quickly; I was doing algebra when most girls are debating whether or not to give up playing with dolls. It was my behavior that baffled them. Like, when I was four, they took me to this hotel in Los Angeles. There was an Olympic-size swimming

pool. I took one look at it, and then I dove headfirst into the deep end. I didn't have the faintest inkling how to swim.

Needless to say, I almost drowned. But that wasn't the disturbing part. The problem was, I dove right back into the deep end the next day. And the next. I'll never forget the look on my father's face every time he fished me out of the warm turquoise water and wagged his long finger in my face with anxious fury. "What is the matter with you?" he kept yelling.

I couldn't answer him. I didn't know.

There were a lot of incidents like that: diving into giant swimming pools, running past the shark warnings into the ocean, walking into traffic, pedaling my tricycle for six miles with no idea how to get back home. . . .

It wasn't until the Agency ran some tests on me that we all discovered that I was missing that pesky little fear gene. Oh, happy day! My ludicrous behavior could finally be explained.

I wasn't stupid. I was fearless.

They'd just confused the two, which, when you think about it, makes perfect sense. I understood what I was doing; I just didn't care about the consequences. So I kept making bad decisions. My ability to reason hadn't caught up with my instincts yet.

And that's really the problem. When you're fearless and you're only acting on instinct, you can do some pretty stupid things. I mean, think about it. How can you make the right choice when you don't even fear the consequences of the wrong one? How can you even tell the difference between right and wrong, between sensible and idiotic?

Yes, there is a point I'm getting to here.

Three minutes ago I had to make a choice. A choice based entirely on instinct. Josh

Kendall and Loki's thugs were coming at me. (How Josh could have been there, given that I'd just seen him shot in the head a few hours earlier, is another story entirely—one I have yet to figure out, and one that is simply too twisted and inexplicable for me to deal with right now. So I will stick to what I understand.) I was basically cornered. And then a car pulled up to the curb, and a man opened the back door, begging me to jump into the car with him where I'd be safe.

I looked at his face, and I had two seconds to decide—was that man my father or my uncle? There was no time for quizzes or close consideration. No time to reason. I looked deep in his eyes, and my gut told me that he was my father. So I got in the car, and we took off down the street.

But I just don't know.

I mean, someone actually capable of experiencing fear would

know better than I would. Did I make the right choice or not? Have my instincts improved with age, or did I just dive into the deep end again? Here I was, sitting in the backseat of the car with my father, and the same thought kept running through my head over and over again:

I should be afraid. I really wish I were afraid right now.

She wanted
to be
shouting,
but her body
was no
longer
capable of
responding
to her
demands.

A Simple Hug

THE CHAOS AND CONFUSION ENDED so suddenly. Gaia couldn't adapt to the serene white noise that took its place. Moments ago, her world had been utter cacophony: the stomps of the enemy closing in on her, the screech of burning rubber on asphalt, the insistent voice of her father (or her uncle) shouting for her to get in the car. Now it was nothing but the cool, sterile interior of a black Mercedes.

But the silence made no difference. Gaia's head was still pounding—her confused thoughts wailing like a jumbo jet in a dizzying tailspin.

She glanced out the window. She hadn't even noticed they were on the FDR Drive. The East River ran just beside the highway, but it was too dark to see by night, especially through the tinted window. The starless sky was as black as the water. Gaia pressed a button to open the window, allowing the dark glass to slide all the way down into the door. Then she leaned forward and closed her eyes, letting the wind pummel her face and eyelids. It roared thunderously in her ears. She hoped to numb her senses, to sandblast away all the horrors of the last twenty-four hours. Maybe the harsh wind could just strip her emotions away layer by layer, until she could no longer feel that rotten crust of guilt and disappointment that was hardening around her like a shell. . . .

Yeah, right. *The Winds of Change*. When was the last time the wind had actually changed anything?

Nothing could alter the facts. Sam was dead. It was still basically her fault. And Ed was drifting further away with every revolution of the car's wheels. If she'd made it into his building before the ambush, she would have asked him to leave with her. Tonight. Immediately. Not to go anyplace specific, but just to *go*. Away from where they were. Not as boyfriend and girlfriend, but not exactly just friends. Just as. . . whatever they were. Or whatever they might become.

It doesn't matter now, she told herself. That imaginary future had been yanked out from under her just as quickly as she'd conjured it up. It was just another dead issue to be tossed into the fire along with all of her other short-lived pipe dreams and useless bursts of optimism. Only her father knew where she was going now. And that was the problem.

He was sitting right beside her, his hands tightly on the wheel, and she had no idea what to say. In the past twenty-four hours, she'd formed every conceivable opinion of him, directed every possible feeling toward him—from unadulterated hatred to desperate concern to utter confusion. His identity had changed in Gaia's mind literally from hour to hour, depending on which lies Loki was feeding her. He'd gone from neglectful father to murder suspect to kidnapper to noble parent. . . in fact, her perceptions had shifted so many times, she found she could barely trust any of her feelings. Even the good ones. She could hardly even bring herself to look at him.

But the longer she avoided him, the more questions she found piling up in her head. Did he know anything else about Sam? Or about Josh, who should have been dead himself but had somehow avoided giving Gaia the satisfaction? Maybe her father had been there when it happened—when Loki and Josh put an end to Sam's innocent life. Was anyone else there for Sam? Had anyone tried to help him? Had he died completely alone?

Suddenly the image of Sam dropping to his knees from a gunshot darted through Gaia's mind. Her body tensed. She couldn't think about it. The guilt was simply too overwhelming. She forced herself to shake it off by leaning further out the window. She opened her mouth as the wind scraped away at her lips and her throat. She couldn't ask her father about Sam. Not yet. The memory was still too fresh, too painful.

But she at least needed to know about her uncle. No one in that Chelsea loft had been able to tell her father and uncle apart—not George, not a gang of agents, not even Gaia herself. One of them had escaped, and one of them had been captured. And if her father was indeed driving, then her uncle—the man she now knew was Loki—was the one they'd cuffed and sent back to jail.

"Where are we going?" she asked finally.

He glanced at her, a faint smile forming at the corners of his mouth. "Just be glad we made it, sweetheart," he said. Slices of light from the passing street lamps flashed across his shadowy face. "Don't worry. I'm taking you someplace safe."

"Yeah, but where?" Gaia persisted. This was no time for cryptic answers. He should know that.

His smile grew larger and more relaxed. "Don't worry," he assured her. He eased up on the gas as they approached Houston Street, pulling off the highway to an abandoned lot. The car lurched to an abrupt halt. He turned to face her. "We're home free, sweetheart. We're free of all of it now. Come here."

He inched closer, opening his arms to her and offering an embrace.

For no reason that Gaia could understand, the gesture made her skin crawl. She stared into his eyes. He *was* her father; she was certain of it. So what was the problem? Had their distance done this much damage? Was her ability to trust him so bruised and battered that the thought of a simple hug had actually come to disgust her? A hug from her dad used to be one of the only three things that could actually cheer her up—the other two being a hug from her mom and chocolate cheesecake. But here was blatant and disheartening proof that her childhood was over. The outstretched arms made her stiff and numb and uneasy.

Still, she knew that she had to respond in kind. They had to start rebuilding their mess of a relationship.

Gaia allowed him to take her in his arms. But a nebulous black thought began to stir in some very remote region of her brain—a thought that was unformed but deeply foreboding. She felt his chin nestled in her neck. His arms were oddly serpentine, sliding across her back and locking her against him. Every part of her wanted to break free from his embrace. The repulsion was palpable. It was almost as if there were a faint inaudible voice buried in her head, trying to dig its way out, trying to tell her something. Her subconscious was sending her images—speaking to her in visual code: She saw herself at four years old, flailing helplessly at the bottom of that sun-drenched light blue swimming pool. She saw herself as a kindergartner, making a beeline for the turbulent ocean, completely ignoring the huge sign that warned of shark-infested waters.

Finally, her inner voice clawed its way to the surface.

You're not certain at all, it whispered. *You've made a mistake.*

Gaia quickly moved to extricate herself—but felt a sharp stinging prick to her arm. "Ow," she hissed. She slapped the spot reflexively. But there was no mosquito or horsefly. As she leaned back she caught a glimpse of something clasped between her father's thumb and forefinger: a long syringe. Her gaze darted to his eyes. One glance confirmed what her subconscious had been trying to tell her all this time. Those were not her father's eyes. And it was not her father's embrace that had repulsed her.

Loki had a set a trap. And Gaia had—fearlessly—jumped right in.

"I'm so sorry, Gaia," he said. "I truly am. I hate having to deceive you." He placed a cap over the syringe and tucked it back in the pocket of his overcoat.

Gaia shook her head. She could only hear him out of her right ear. The left ear was clogged with static. A second later the right ear started closing up as well. Her uncle was beginning to look two-dimensional, as if he were blending into the black background of the car's interior.

"Stop the car," Gaia shouted.

Only. . . she wasn't shouting. She wanted to be shouting, but her body was no longer capable of responding to her demands. "Stop the car," she repeated. The words were no more than a whisper. Her lips had gone numb, as had the rest of her face.

"It's just a sedative," Loki said gently, leaning towards her again. "I'm so sorry, Gaia, but I had no choice. I know how little you trust me now, and I had to get you away from Tom somehow. Just rest now, sweetheart. When you wake up, you'll be safe, and I'll explain everything."

"Stop. . . ," Gaia began again, but she was unable to complete the sentence. She focused every ounce of energy on her eyelids. She had to keep them open, no matter how heavy they might feel. She was a fighter. She would not lose consciousness. She couldn't. Her body fell helplessly back against the seat.

Stay awake, Gaia! she screamed silently. *Fight it.*

This sensation was different from the blackouts that always followed her fights. It was more aggressive. Insistent. Her iron will crumbled even as she pleaded was with her body to attack, to pounce. . . to hurl her uncle's body through the window. But she could hardly make herself blink.

"I know you don't believe me," he said. He ran a hand gently down her paralyzed cheek. "I swear this is all for your own good. This is all because I love you. I'll prove it to you, Gaia. Just have patience."

The light dimmed. He was rapidly disappearing—his face now little more than a silhouette. Gaia's eyelids fluttered. It had a nauseating strobe effect on what was left of her vision.

Stay awake, she screamed at herself again. *Stay—*

But before she could complete the thought, her consciousness faded completely.

The Obvious Maybe

WAITING FOR GAIA HAD BEGUN TO make Ed Fargo feel as if he'd been beamed into one of those insane-asylum movies. *One Flew Over the Fargo's Nest.* Or maybe *Ed, Interrupted.* So he'd forced himself out on another night walk. But of course, that only made him feel worse. Given that Gaia could be beaten up and lying in any alley or gutter, it didn't really help to take a leisurely tour of alleys and gutters—which, at three in the morning, pretty much stood out as the defining features of downtown New York City.

About eight blocks into the walk, Ed suddenly realized that he was being an idiot. What the hell was he doing eight blocks from home? Gaia might be collapsing at his door this very second—just as she had the night before. And here he was, out for an evening stroll. He quickly reversed himself and started crutching back toward his building as fast possible, nearly pole-vaulting across the sidewalk. . . looking very much like just another loony out on the streets in the middle of the night.

He never should have let her go after Sam by herself. That had been his first mistake. (Well, not really—it had actually been about his thousandth mistake in the past forty-eight hours.) But true to Amazonian form, Gaia had insisted that she handle everything on her own. Since then, he'd been doing everything in his power to maintain a sense of humor and stave off the panic, but he couldn't. Not anymore. Sleep deprivation alone was tearing him to shreds.

She'd left him more than eight hours ago. He hadn't heard one word from her since. He'd run through stacks and stacks of maybes in his head. Maybe she never found her uncle or her father, and she'd finally forced herself to skip town. Maybe she found Sam and rescued him and they'd run off together for a life of wild romance on some Caribbean Island. Maybe the whole Sam kidnapping was a hoax or a practical joke or something, and now she and Sam and her father and her uncle were laughing about the whole thing over a couple of cold ones. . . .

Each maybe had to be more ludicrous than the last. It had to be crazy enough to keep Ed's mind occupied; otherwise he would have to consider the most obvious maybe. The maybe he'd been dreading and avoiding for the last three hours. The maybe he had to avoid at all costs. Allowing it to enter his mind would be like voluntarily submitting himself to Chinese water-torture. He'd just finally confessed to being completely in love with her—and she'd *promised* him that she would be back. They still had a conversation to finish. Ed had to believe that Gaia kept every one of her promises. Of course. He knew she did.

But that thought only served to bring Ed right back to the worst-case scenario.

Given that Gaia kept all her promises; given that only a sadist would let Ed pour his guts out, then leave him hanging without a word. . . there was no way her disappearance could have been by choice. None at all.

By the time the reached the lobby, Ed was drenched in sweat. He practically fell into his elevator, panting until it opened on his floor. Then he dashed to the apartment. He left the key in the lock as he swung open the door.

"Gaia?" he called out hopefully. "Gaia, are you here?"

Silence.

Ed paused in the middle of his living room. She wasn't here. He had no idea what to do. He should call someone—the cops, Heather, even his parents upstate (wherever the hell they were). But all he could do was stand there in the oppressive and ugly quiet. The apartment had never felt so empty. He'd always loved having the place to himself, but now that Gaia had lived with him for a day, it felt wrong without her. As far as Ed was concerned, it had already become her home, too.

And he was getting the distinct feeling that she would not be coming home.

The most obvious maybe. . . The thought of it began weighing him down, crushing him toward the floor like excess gravity, causing his shaky legs to ache and nearly buckle from the pressure. All the wishes and fantasies and complicated scenarios faded away. There was really only one thought that remained.

Just please be alive, he prayed silently.

He could survive if she didn't love him the way he loved her. He could survive if she ran off with Sam. He could even somehow survive if he never saw her again. Barely—as long as he knew she was all right. But if Gaia hadn't survived, then neither could he. It was as simple as that.

Contradictory Purposes

WHITE CEILING. BRIGHT LIGHT.

The room darted in and out of focus like a television on the fritz. As she crept back into consciousness, Gaia tried to gather as many visual details as possible. But she could still only keep her eyes open for a few seconds at a time. Her head was lolling. It felt as if it had been filled with rubber cement and left to dry. The need for sleep was more powerful than any other force on earth. She was sitting somewhere. . . .

Flowered vase. Silver candlestick holders. Medical tray. Latex gloves. The random images weren't adding up. *Moroccan rug. Mahogany desk. Scalpels. Syringes. Two microscopes.* Was she in a medical lab or a living room? Or was she still asleep?

She tried to massage her temples. She couldn't move her hands. Once again she forced her eyes to flutter open—and even though the dry, stinging retinas begged to be tucked back under the lids, she fought back. Gradually, her vision adjusted to the blinding sunlight from the windows behind her. Her paralyzed hands swam into focus. No. . . they weren't paralyzed. They were restrained, strapped firmly to the arms of her chair with two buckles. Her feet were restrained too, ankles bound against the front legs of her chair. She used what little strength she had to try to wrench her wrists free of the restraints, but it was pointless. Her resistance only served to cut off the circulation, turning her flesh different shades of purple and crimson.

She was trapped.

Any remotely normal person would have been terrified

at this point. Strapped down. Vulnerable to anything and everything that Loki had in mind—grotesque genetic experiments, mutilation, torture. She might as well have been blindfolded, given a cigarette, and placed in front of the firing line. She was, for all intents and purposes, dead. Without fear to occupy her mind, however, all Gaia could feel was sickeningly angry. And groggy. And most of all, foolish.

She'd gathered such a vast wealth of knowledge in her short life. She could match wits with experts on any number of topics—calculus, chaos theory, Eastern European history, molecular biology. . . but her instincts? Without fear to inform her decisions, her instincts were still those of a goddamn four-year-old. She could have taken on Josh and those goons. She could have taken them all on. Why the hell had she gotten in that car? Why couldn't she *see* that it was Loki and not her father? Why—

The sound of a turning doorknob put her questions on hold.

Gaia raised her bleary eyes, watching as her uncle stepped quietly into the room, like a concerned father trying not to wake his baby. She wondered for a moment just how deeply deranged he might be. His look of concern was repulsive. But the moment he saw her, his expression shifted. His eyes narrowed. His lips tensed into a livid scowl. He ducked his head back behind the door and spat out some inaudible complaint.

"Now!" he finished. "Get in here now!"

Two faceless thugs—as nondescript and familiar as every other she'd encountered—rushed into the room and dropped to their knees directly in front of her.

"Get them off," Loki barked. "I never said to use the restraints." He turned to Gaia. "I'm so sorry," he murmured gently. His ability to completely change his demeanor from one moment to the next was disturbing, fascinating. But this was hardly the time to indulge in a psychological profile. She had to size up the situation and figure a way out of it.

Her senses were still slightly numb, but she could feel the thugs' thick, callused fingers digging into her skin as they tugged at her restraints and unbuckled them. Finally the blood flowed freely through her wrists. Strength surged back into her limbs. Yes, she was coming out of it now—all the while taking mental notes for a potential escape. The men untying her were armed with nine-millimeter pistols. Not a surprise.

Gaia turned back towards her uncle and studied his eyes suspiciously. She couldn't help but wonder if Loki hadn't prearranged this little episode with the restraints. It did, after all, seem to serve

Loki's two very contradictory purposes perfectly. He could present himself as the caring father figure, insisting that they "free" his niece. That would demonstrate his "compassion." But without ever openly threatening her, he could also send a very clear message: she was free to run, but there was no point in trying to escape.